Morag would have enjoyed going back to
Wharuaroa, where she had been happy
as a teenager, if it hadn't meant coming
into constant contact with Thorpe
Cunningham, who couldn't forget how
she had—as he thought—treated his
brother so badly. But why was she so
anxious that Thorpe should think well
of her? Wasn't it all water under the
bridge?

SHADOW OF THE PAST

BY

ROBYN DONALD

MILLS & BOON LIMITED
17–19 FOLEY STREET
LONDON W1A 1DR

First published 1979
Australian copyright 1979
Philippine copyright 1979
This edition 1979

© Robyn Donald 1979

ISBN 0 263 73097 2

Set in Linotype Baskerville 10 on 11½ pt.

Made and printed in Great Britain by
Richard Clay (The Chaucer Press), Ltd., Bungay, Suffolk

CHAPTER ONE

GETTING three pre-school children, their convalescing mother and a vast mountain of baggage from Christchurch to Kerikeri was, Morag Nelson decided, quite the most exhausting exercise she had ever mounted in her life as a Karitane nurse. At least they didn't have to change planes, and the baby had slept all of the way on her mother's lap, leaving Morag to cope with Jason and Richie, the three-year-old twins. They were a handful, but fortunately this was their first flight, so they were somewhat in awe of the whole procedure, which made coping with them a little easier.

'Nearly there,' she promised now, as the glittering expanse of water which was the Bay of Islands appeared on their right. 'Look, boys—there's the sea.'

'The sea—the sea!' Richie crowed, while his brother added, 'See the sea, Morag. See the sea, Richie!'

Morag nodded, awed by the beauty of it. A sudden film of moisture blurred her vision. Surreptitiously she blinked, wondering why the sight of the bay should make her homesick for the first time ever. After an absence of six years it seemed rather ironic, especially as she had shaken the dust of this part of northern New Zealand from her feet with unmitigated joy, vowing never to come back.

Well, here she was, and heading furthermore straight into the lion's den. A swift glance at Richie's absorbed face brought the sick feeling back into her stomach, the feeling she had had ever since his mother had announced that she hated Christchurch without her husband and was going back home to stay with her brother.

Who just happened to be Thorpe Cunningham. Who just happened to have thrown Morag out of Wharuaroa six long years ago, ordering her never to darken his doors again in the approved manner. They were alike, he and his nephew, but what in Richie was a bony unchildlike face had suffered a sea-change in his uncle, turning him into a startlingly handsome man, if you liked big men with dark copper hair and hard, blue-green eyes. For herself, Morag didn't, and it was not entirely due to his reaction to the knowledge that his brother was determined to marry her. The antagonism between them had been instant and inexplicable, made worse by the fact that Graham had fallen in love with her seventeen-year-old self, but it had not been caused by that knowledge.

If she cared to she could summon up that last scene without closing her eyes. He had stopped his car on the side of the road, almost forcing her and her bicycle into the ditch, then came out of it like a beast of prey, his expression so black that she had been terrified.

Without preamble he had demanded, 'Are you pregnant?'

Her temper had fired to meet his. 'No, I am *not*! And you've got a nerve——'

'Shut up. I thought as much. Girls like you don't get pregnant, do they? Well, how much do you want?'

And when she had gaped he had repeated harshly, 'Don't try to look innocent, Morag. How much will it cost me to get rid of you?'

'I don't want your money,' she flashed indignantly.

'You don't want Graham, either. Oh, I've watched you. He wants you, all right, but you're distinctly luke-warm.'

Which was true enough. She wasn't in love with

Graham, but she didn't know how to break things off without hurting him—and anyway, she thought, marriage to him couldn't be any worse than her present life. She hated being wardmaid in the little cottage hospital—or perhaps she was jealous because her own dream, to take care of children, was impossible. To become a Karitane nurse you needed money to keep yourself over the first twenty months, and there was no way that her aunt and uncle would fork out for that. So marriage to Graham and her own children to care for seemed some sort of alternative.

'Well?'

Afterwards she never knew how she had managed to find the nerve to say coolly, 'Actually, I wouldn't mind some money.'

'I thought so,' he said, a note of satisfaction running through his voice. 'How much?'

Arrogant beast, Morag said to herself as aloud she named an impossible sum.

His dark brows drew together, but without saying anything he reached into his hip pocket and drew out a cheque book. On the long bonnet of his car he wrote the cheque, ripped it out and handed it to her, his contempt clearly evinced by the twist of those hard lips.

Almost she had torn the cheque up in front of him, but she had been humiliated this far, she would not back down now. 'Thank you,' she said coolly, hoping that he would attribute the shakiness of her voice to triumph.

'Not so fast.' This time he used the back of an envelope to scribble on. 'Sign this.'

Nausea clogged her throat, but she read on doggedly. 'I, Morag Nelson, promise that in return for the sum of money I received from Thorpe Cunningham I will leave Wharuaroa for Auckland or further south and will not attempt to contact Graham Cunningham in any way ever again.' He had dated it, and now, without comment, was holding his pen towards her.

It was an expensive pen, making her signature something almost impressive, she thought, but she had felt smirched and beaten, degraded by his cynical appraisal of the situation and her acceptance of his bribe as she signed the humiliating thing.

'Don't go to sleep, Richie,' she said now, running her hand across the dark copper hair. 'Look, we're coming to land. If you look out you'll see all the orange trees in the orchards.'

This had the effect of checking his drowsiness. Kerikeri was a citrus-growing area and from the air the neat rows of trees marched in regimented order behind the windbreaks of bamboo and Japanese cedar and tall Australian eucalypts. Morag pointed out the roads, the streams which found their way down into the Kerikeri Inlet and thence into the Bay of Islands, and the green paddocks of the dairy and sheep farms which surrounded the fruit-growing area.

'Where does Uncle Thorpe live?' Jason asked.

Morag gestured inland. 'In those hills, love. Quite a way from Kerikeri in a place called Wharuaroa.'

He tried to get his tongue around the word and chuckled when he failed. '*That's* a big word. I forgot it.'

'Yes, it means the long valley. Your uncle's house is built overlooking the valley.'

'Have you been there?' That was Richie withdrawing his eyes from the view outside the window to stare curiously at her.

'Yes, I've been there.'

He nodded, turning the fact over in his brain, then asked, 'Do you know my uncle?'

'Yes. At least I used to, when I was young.' For some

reason this made both boys chuckle. They were still laughing when the plane touched down at the little airport just outside Kerikeri.

In the business of getting everybody out of the plane Morag forgot to be nervous. Sally Johnston had gone very pale. Her descent was made clinging to a steward's arm while Morag took baby Rachel and the two boys and made her way down on to the concrete. It was almost dark, for the plane arrived after five and as it was winter the wind whipped around their legs with a chill reminder of the season. At least, it wasn't anywhere near as cold as Christchurch had been, Morag thought gratefully, pulling the shawl around the baby, while her eyes searched the cluster of people who waited beyond the gate.

Yes, he was there, standing against a big red car. Quite suddenly Morag remembered the cold sea-colour of his eyes and felt a return of the old sick fear. Then the baby began to whimper and Jason whined, 'I'm cold!' and she thought to herself that six years had made a great difference to her. Her responsible job had given her confidence and self-assurance. And if he cut up rough—well, she would leave and see how he would like looking after his sister's children!

'Oh—*Thorpe*!' Sally Johnston cried, as if he were her last remaining link with humanity.

'Sally?' His voice was deep, somewhat grim, his glance swift and all-encompassing as he scooped his sister into the car before turning back to the others.

There could be no mistaking the recognition in his eyes. They narrowed, became intent and hard, then he said, 'Miss Nelson, isn't it? Morag Nelson?'

'Yes.'

'Hop in. Those children look tired.'

And just how to take that she didn't know, but apparently he wasn't going to refuse to let her soil the carpet in his car with the touch of her feet. At least, she thought defiantly, she had paid him back every cent of the money he had given her. She could hold her head high.

The humming of the car engine put Rachel and the twins to sleep almost immediately. Morag looked down at their trustful faces and felt her heart contract even though she knew that it would be far better not to allow herself to become emotionally involved with her charges. They were so tired that there would probably be tears and tantrums when they woke up at Wharua-roa, and Sally, in her present state, would be no help.

She could hear her now, the tired voice plaintive.

'I hope it isn't too much bother, Thorpe, but I felt so *wretched* after this bout of 'flu and I wanted to come home.'

'There's no reason why you shouldn't,' he replied evenly. 'Hazel is in high gig at the thought of having children to spoil.'

Sally smiled. 'Oh, Morag won't let them be spoiled. When you lived here, Morag,' turning to include her in the conversation—'whereabouts was your home?'

'Just down the road from Wharuaroa—about two miles away.'

Thorpe said calmly, 'Her uncle bought Sam Otaki's dairy farm, Sally. That would be after you went away to school.'

'Oh, yes,' Sally nodded. 'I wondered why I didn't recognise you, but of course I wasn't at home much after that. How is Graham, Thorpe, and his Louise?'

'Very well, both of them.' Pitching his voice so that it carried into the back of the car, he continued, 'Graham has been married for a couple of years, Morag.

His wife is English; he went over there—oh, it must have been after you left.'

'Oh? I hadn't heard.'

'Ah well, one loses touch easily enough, I suppose.' This was said with a certain grim note of warning.

Resisting the childish temptation to stick her tongue out at the back of his head, Morag contented herself with murmuring, 'Yes, one does,' and as the two in the front continued their conversation in lower voices she was able to look around without appearing rude.

They were climbing steadily towards the hills which sheltered the Cunningham station. Behind them lay the waters of the Bay of Islands and the rich citrus area, ahead and on either side were big farms whose rolling green paddocks were cut by heavily wooded gullies. Shelter belts of pines and macrocarpas as well as the beautiful native puriri trees protected them from the South. Morag loved Christchurch and the South Island, but as the quick winter darkness fell she felt a sudden sense of homecoming, in spite of Thorpe Cunningham in the front seat.

Wharuaroa was the name of the station, also of the valley itself, a long, wide river valley lying north and south with the Puri stream running through it. The station took in the hills to the south and west as well as a fair proportion of the river flats, but as they came through the cleft of the hills overlooking the valley Morag saw the lights of the other homesteads scattered down the valley on either side of the road. One would be where she had spent four miserable years with her aunt and uncle. She had felt no grief when they were drowned shortly after she left Wharuaroa, for they had made no attempt to give her the love she needed as the orphaned daughter of Kate Warren's sister; a sense of duty, Morag had often felt, was a bad thing to have. She had been quite happy in the orphanage, but Aunt Kate had said no relation of hers was going to live on public charity.

So they had brought her here and she had never been allowed to forget that she lived on their charity, until Thorpe Cunningham provided the money for her escape.

Gently moving Jason's head along her arm, she thought wryly that Wharuaroa had not been a happy place for her, or for her aunt and uncle, drowned in a boating accident because her uncle had never seen the necessity for lifejackets.

So Graham was married! He would be—oh, twenty-seven now, for he had been just twenty-one that summer when he had wanted to marry her. Looking back she could see them, a couple of kids playing at being grown-up, trading stolen kisses and high romantic dreams until big brother came along and quite efficiently put an end to their idyll. If Graham was that age then Thorpe would be thirty-one and Sally must be twenty-six; ironic that the place should bring back these snippets of information. She hadn't thought of any of them for years. In Wharuaroa the Cunninghams were the big people, the station owners. Their children went to boarding school, they holidayed in the ski-fields of the Southern Alps or overseas, and invitations to a function there meant that you had arrived socially in the district.

Rural New Zealand, she thought, and tolerantly, why not? They were a cultured family from what she could remember; at least Thorpe's mother had had pretensions that way. The station was well farmed, the family was worthy of respect. And in spite of Thorpe's refusal to contemplate any marriage plans between her and Graham, she doubted if he was a snob. Merely practical, and sensible. And a few other things, like ruthless and overbearing and arrogantly confident of himself.

The rattle of the cattle-stop made the twins stir, but Rachel slept on, getting heavier and heavier on Morag's arm. When the car had drawn up outside the double-panelled doors of the homestead she said to Thorpe as he opened the door to the back: 'Could you take Jason, please. Mrs Johnston, can you carry the baby? Then I'll take Richard and with any luck we'll get them inside before an outburst.'

He lifted his brows at her cool assumption of authority but did as he was asked, so that within a moment they were in a wide hall where a plump, almost middle-aged woman was cooing and clucking.

'Let's get them upstairs,' Sally urged. 'Hazel, you can admire them tomorrow. If all goes well, they'll sleep right on through.'

The house had been built in the palmy days of the cattle barons, so it possessed a nursery suite, consisting of two small bedrooms and a playroom as well as a bathroom. While Morag skilfully undressed the boys, Sally fed her daughter and when they finally left, all was peacefully silent.

Outside, in the hallway, Morag said, 'Listen, I'll stay with them tonight in case they wake. You need your sleep!'

'Do I ever!' Sally sighed, leaning against the wall as she pushed a hand through her pale red hair. 'Honestly, devoted though I am to my errant husband, I could kill him for this! He just has no right to head off for the South Pole for six months and leave me, even in your capable hands!'

"Flu does leave you like that,' Morag agreed, feeling suddenly much older than her employer. 'You should go straight to bed, you know. You look almost worn out.'

'Yes, I suppose I should.' Sally looked her indecision for a moment before turning to open a door behind her. 'Look, here's your room, next door to the nursery suite. Like it? There's a connecting door, so you don't have to go out into the hall to get from A to B.' She cast a swift glance around, wrinkling her nose in dismay. 'Hell's teeth, it's a bit upper servant, isn't it? The rest of the place was redecorated some years ago, but this looks as though it's never been touched.'

Chuckling, Morag bounced on the bed. 'That's O.K.,' she said with satisfaction. 'The rest can be as awful as you like, providing the bed is comfortable—first commandment in a Karitane's bible. Actually, I rather like this room. It's got character.'

'Well, at least it's clean,' her employer said without satisfaction. 'Oh, there's your bag. Use the nursery bathroom, Morag, and then come on down. If the routine is the same as always we'll gather in the parlour about seven for sherry. And light conversation.'

Morag got to her feet, making up her mind with quick decision. 'Do you mind if I don't come down?'

'Oh—why?'

'Because if the kids wake they could be frightened in a strange place.' Morag smiled with irony, 'I wouldn't relax. And they *are* my job.'

Sally's answering look was shrewd, but after a moment she nodded. 'Fair enough. I'd like to crawl into bed myself, but I'll feel better after a bath and new face. And Thorpe would be disappointed—at least, not disappointed. A little scornful, perhaps, for being such a weak thing. He's made of iron, so he thinks everyone else is too.'

Left alone, Morag looked around the room, smiling to herself. Sally's taste ran to exquisitely crafted antiques, so naturally she despised the clean scrubbed lines of the solid kauri furniture in the room; even the patchwork quilt had evoked no appreciation from her. But the room had a quaint cottagey feel to it which Morag liked, and it was comfortable even to the old bentwood rocker in one corner. And it was warm! Whoever had modernised the homestead hadn't forgotten the central heating.

She bathed and unpacked, slipping into a pale blue dress which contrasted with her dark hair and blue eyes and was not in the least revealing. Practically the first thing one learnt when one left the Karitane hospital was that revealing clothes were definitely not welcome on the job. Consequently her wardrobe was restrained, almost prim, except for a few things she had bought to wear in between jobs. Paying back Thorpe Cunningham had taken most of her spare money, so her wardrobe contained nothing spectacular, certainly not in the same league as Sally's. But then Thorpe Cunningham's sister could afford the very best in clothes to show off her titian beauty.

Not that Morag envied her. Perhaps, she thought as she moved around her room, perhaps I've grown too fond of my independence, but I'm so glad I've got it! In a way this trip back to Wharuaroa was like an exorcism for her, ridding her of all traces of guilt and grief and humiliation left over from the years she had spent here. She felt renewed, almost cleansed, as though she could meet Thorpe Cunningham on the same level and not ever have to fear his anger or contempt again.

Humming, she went into the nursery to check on the children, and there he was, big and dark in the dim light, looking down at Jason with a remote shuttered expression.

At the movement of the door he looked up, his features becoming so forbidding and arrogant that Morag felt she should drop a curtsey. Pride held her shoulders straight; she tucked Richie's hand beneath the covers, checked Rachel in the crib, and looked Jason over. Then she stood, her hands at her sides, watching him.

Not much to her surprise he inclined his head at the communicating door, then followed her through it, demanding as soon as he had closed it behind him, 'Might I ask what the *hell* you're doing here?'

'Looking after the children,' she answered quietly, determined not to lose her temper or her assurance. He was far too large for her room.

Without thinking she retreated behind the bed, her defences up and impregnable.

'Don't play games with me.'

The words were softly spoken but the threat was clear. Against her will Morag swallowed, the muscles working convulsively beneath the pale skin of her throat.

After a moment he continued, 'I want you out of here as fast as you can go.'

Anger warmed the cool blue depths of her eyes, brought a flush to her cheekbones. 'That's up to you, of course. But I hope you'll explain to Mrs Johnston just why you're sacking me.'

'I'll do exactly that,' he said softly, eyeing her with a contempt which seared the confidence from her as if it had never existed, as if she was still seventeen and unable to protect herself against his harshness.

Shrugging, fighting for control, she said, 'Very well, then.'

'No further protests?'

She shook her head. 'No. You won't even need to offer me money this time. I have no difficulty getting jobs now.'

Frowning, he looked sharply across the bed at her. 'Then I conclude that I may have difficulty getting another nurse to help my sister?'

'You probably will find it very difficult.'

His frown deepened, the autocratic features set in lines of deep displeasure. In spite of his quite stunning good looks he was not the sort of man to appeal to Morag, although even in her innocent youth she had been well aware of his reputation. To her he was eminently resistable, she thought, flippancy coming to her rescue to hide the fact that her heart seemed to be beating double time in her throat.

'I see.' He came to a decision, looked at her with a chilling dislike which reinforced the meaning of his words.

'I'll ring Auckland tomorrow, and if I have no success you can stay. But one false step and you'll be out of here so fast that Sally won't have time to say goodbye.'

'Would you care to tell me what constitutes a false step?' she queried curtly, the deep blue of her glance as cold as his.

'To start off with, you'll leave Graham alone.' Her astonishment must have been quite open, but he gave no signs of recognising it.

'As you pointed out the last time we met,' she retorted, 'I didn't love him then. I can assure you that the six years since then have made me quite indifferent to him. I came here to do a job. I intend to do just that, and no more.'

He smiled with rare irony at her words, his arctic

gaze travelling with insolent thoroughness over her body, finally coming to rest on her face. 'You were a catalyst here before,' he said drily. 'I see no reason to suppose you'll be any different this time. Just remember what I said.'

And he was gone, moving as silently as the beast of prey she had fancifully likened him to. Morag stared after him, her brain in a whirl. A catalyst? From her chemistry at school she knew what a catalyst was, but why should he think of her as an agent who precipitates action without being touched by it herself? And that last appraisal had been downright rude, she thought indignantly. He had looked her over as if she was a woman he was buying for the night, assessing her desirability with crude directness which surely was unlike him?

Disposing herself in the rocking chair, she leaned back against the smooth wood, her eyes closed as she tried to remember what she had heard about Thorpe Cunningham when she had lived at Wharuaroa.

Not all that much. Aunt Kate dealt in innuendoes rather than straight gossip, but his name had been linked with various women. None from the valley, so he didn't go around seducing the local girls in old baronial fashion. But from somewhere she had gained the knowledge that he was greatly sought after by women and that he wasn't above accepting what was so freely offered. It must have been Graham who told her, though they talked little about the older brother Graham hated. But even though he hated him he had never hinted that Thorpe was a greedy sensualist, yet that appraisal had been as direct an insult as any open proposition.

The mirror on the wardrobe door was a good Victorian one. It reflected Morag clearly, without distortions, as she reviewed herself gravely in its depths.

Really, nothing spectacular. Hair of that blackness which has blue lights in it, skin a trifle too pale for her dark lashes and hair, eyes deep blue and not too revealing. Her features were neat but not in the least stunning, a mouth generously curved, too wide for beauty above a chin which was determined and had been called obstinate. Usually by men who had found her old-fashioned principles annoying, she mused, and wondered whether her trim, slim figure had anything to do with their attempts to coax her into bed with them.

Shrugging, she turned away, annoyed with herself for allowing one assessing stare from Thorpe Cunningham to affect her like that. That he was rude she had always known, and if he cared to behave like a boor that was his business. If she gave him no openings he would have to content himself with looking!

But why on earth should he warn her off Graham, unless he was paranoid about his brother? Or, she thought shrewdly, unless Graham's marriage was not particularly happy. Whatever, she had no intention of allowing herself to be again drawn into the affairs of the Cunninghams. They epitomised a time of her life she would rather forget.

Of course, if she had had any sense of self-preservation at all she would have refused to accompany Sally up here as soon as she realised who her employer was and where she intended to go. Unfortunately it seemed that compassion was a good deal stronger that any selfish desire for peace of mind, she thought wryly as she pulled her diary from her bag and sat down at the desk to write it up.

A tap on the door heralded her dinner, borne somewhat ungraciously by the woman they had called

Hazel. The housekeeper, Morag assumed.

Realising that she was going to have to placate her if she wanted any co-operation, Morag jumped to her feet.

'You shouldn't have gone to all this trouble,' she said quickly. 'I could have come down.'

The older woman permitted herself a slight easing of the severe lines of her face. 'Well, it *is* inconvenient, but of course you're right to want to keep within hearing of the children. Especially this first night. How are they?'

'Sound asleep.' Morag gestured towards the communicating door. 'Like to have a peep at them?'

There was no stiffness now. Eagerly Hazel preceded Morag into the nursery, and stood for a long moment looking down at them. To her intense surprise Morag noticed tears glittering in the older woman's eyes.

'Well, they have grown,' Hazel said after a moment. Back in Morag's room she blew her nose and said defiantly, 'I'm a sentimental idiot, but sleeping children *get* me. Soldier and I only had the one, and he's grown up and gone now; some day he'll give me some grandchildren, and they're going to be the most spoiled kids south of the Equator!'

Morag wondered whether it might pay to suggest that the Johnston kids didn't need any extra spoiling, but decided to wait. It would be stupid to antagonise her so early on in the piece. If necessary she would be able to cope with a doting housekeeper, as she had coped with doting grandmothers before.

Anyway, the food was delicious, soup and lamb *noisettes* with vegetables so fresh that they must have been grown on the place, and for dessert a tamarillo concoction with thick cream which reminded Morag that she was back in the sub-tropical north and could expect such delicacies as the tart, ruby-red tamarillos, green feijoas which tasted like a delicious mixture of pineapple and guava, and the hairy, pale brown kiwi-fruit with their lime green flesh and sumptuous flavour.

After the meal she slipped downstairs with her tray, finding her way by instinct to the kitchen where Hazel and a big, suntanned, inarticulate man were eating.

'Good?' Hazel asked with the anxiety of a true cook.

'Superb!'

Which brought a satisfied smile. 'There's coffee in the pot if you want it. Oh,' waving at the man beside her, 'this is Soldier, my husband.'

'How do you do?' Solemnly Morag and he shook hands, then he asked her about the trip up before falling to at his meal with the appetite of a man to whom hard physical labour is normal.

'No, no coffee, thanks,' Morag told the housekeeper. 'I'll pop back up just in case one of them wakes.'

She had never been inside the homestead before; when Graham had courted her they had met secretly, so she looked around her with admiring interest as she walked through the ground floor. Somehow these old houses with their mixtures of styles and periods had something that no amount of money could buy, she thought, remembering the exquisitely decorated home of a business entrepreneur which, by comparison to this, had been cold and unfriendly.

This furniture, those paintings and that superb Japanese vase had been bought because someone loved them and they had been placed so that they showed to their best advantage. They all looked happy together, Morag decided as she ascended the wide, beautifully carved kauri staircase.

No one stirred when she did a final check after her bath in the minuscule bathroom. It was early, but she couldn't fight off sleep for much longer, and when for the third time her eyelids drooped over the same sentence in her book she turned the light off and crept gratefully back into the bed's warm embrace.

It was a still, cold night. Perhaps there would be a frost in the morning, but only a light one, for this was the north. Somewhere outside a lamb baaed plaintively. A morepork called from the trees in the gully nearby, the little owl's cry resounding out over the valley. A long distance away another answered it. Smiling, Morag turned over and went to sleep.

Rachel woke at six o'clock, her demanding wails coming from a long way away to Morag's sleepy ears. It took her a moment to wake, then she leaped out of bed and went in to pick the baby up before her cries woke the boys. After changing her Morag slipped out into the corridor to take her to her mother to be fed.

Sally was in the next bedroom, a very luxurious affair in blues and greens which was a perfect frame for her Titian colouring. She was still sound asleep, her cheek pillowed in her hand, not even waking to Morag's tap at the door.

Feeling like a slavedriver, Morag said, 'Sally—Mrs Johnston. Wake up! Here's Rachel.'

There was a convulsive movement from beneath the sheets, then the long lashes fluttered and lifted, to stare at Morag and the squirming Rachel without recognition.

'What——' she muttered, and then yawned. 'Oh—oh, *Morag*, how could you! I'd just welcomed Sandy home from the South Pole!'

Grinning, Morag tucked Rachel in beside her mother. 'Well, go back to sleep. Rachel won't mind. Or if you like I'll make you a cup of tea.'

Fondly Sally gazed into the hungry face of her

daughter, a smile of sleepy pleasure curving her sensitive mouth. 'A cup of tea would be lovely. Come on,
piglet, drink up.'

There was no equipment for tea-making in the
nursery, so Morag climbed into slacks and a blouse
before setting off down the stairs towards the kitchen.
It was still dark, but a three-quarters moon sent suffi-
cient light in through the windows for her to find her
way about without having to search for light switches.

Once in the kitchen she set about filling the kettle,
moving as quietly as she could to prevent waking anyone else, her expression remote and absorbed as she
found a tray, a small teapot, two cups and saucers and
took milk from the huge double-doored refrigerator.
As she waited for the kettle to boil she looked round
appreciatively. Whoever had renovated this kitchen
had been clever as well as practical. The old wood range
still stood, glossily black, in its alcove. No doubt it had
been banked last night and only needed a blow on the
embers to set it going again. It would heat water and
keep the kitchen regions warm as well as coping with
the cooking. Morag thought of Soldier's muscles and
decided that chopping wood to keep this thing going
was probably cause for most of them.

The rest of the place was a most attractive mixture
of modernity and tradition, from the big pottery crocks
which no doubt held pickles to the huge electric stove
and refrigerator. Hazel was a very lucky woman, Morag
mused, pouring water over the tea-leaves.

It was a little harder manoeuvring her way back up
the stairs with the tray, but she managed it, only to
almost drop the thing when someone switched the light
on from the top.

It did not need the prickling of the hair on the back
of her neck to tell her who the someone was.

'Good morning,' she said cheerfully, determined to be pleasant if it killed her.

Her employer's brother was dressed in a robe and nothing else, it appeared from the one swift glance she gave him. Such informal attire brought a faint flush to her cheekbones. He must have noticed it, for there was a hint of hateful mockery in his deep tones when he responded to her greeting.

'Good morning, Morag. Would you like me to take that?'

'No, thank you.'

'In future,' he suggested smoothly, 'it would be easier if you use the lights.'

'Now that I know where they are I certainly shall. If,' she said with cool composure, 'there are any future occasions.'

'Ah, yes.' He fell into step beside her, apparently not in the least embarrassed by his lack of clothing. 'I've reconsidered my decision. Sally speaks very highly of you, and I doubt if you're any longer a risk to Graham.'

Morag had the usual reaction to being patronised, so for a moment she seriously considered telling him just what he could do with her job. Startled by the strength of her resentment, she subdued it, knowing very well that she could not leave Sally in the lurch. With what she hoped was commendable restraint she said nothing, although the tray trembled as her fingers grasped it tightly.

'But,' he resumed, 'I meant what I said last night. No tricks, or you go, and I'll make sure that you never get a job in a decent home again.'

They were almost at Sally's door. Turning to face him, Morag lifted her mutinous gaze to rake his handsome features scathingly. 'You needn't worry,' she almost hissed. 'I don't believe in breaking up marriages, Mr Cunningham, so that leaves only you for me to exercise my fatal fascination on. Believe me, I'd rather die!'

His brows lifted in such complete disbelief that she stepped back, sickened by his arrogant inflexibility.

'You thought nothing of trying your 'prentice hand on Graham,' he returned viciously. 'I don't believe that leopards change their spots.'

'So that I'm damned eternally in your eyes?'

He gave her an oddly hesitant glance for one so compellingly sure of himself, then said harshly, 'Let's just say that it would take some doing for me to change my mind. I know your type, Morag. Efficient, good at your job, trustworthy in most respects, yet always with an eye out for the main chance.'

'Thank you,' she said with a glittering smile. 'I could favour you with a character reading, too, but I'm too polite. Now, if you *don't* mind, your sister likes a cup of tea while she's feeding the baby. And she likes it *hot*!'

CHAPTER TWO

'WAS that Thorpe?'

Morag nodded, keeping her back to Sally as she poured the tea. 'Yes.'

'He's always up at the crack of dawn. Um, that looks lovely, Morag. Did he shock you with his lack of clothes?'

'He had a robe on,' Morag said almost defensively, walking across to the window to twitch the curtain aside so that she could look into the gathering dawn.

Sally's chuckle was sly yet companionable. 'Thorpe doesn't give a hoot what people think, bless him. He was the one stable thing in our life after Dad died and Mum got all wrapped up in art and artists. Then she died, but Thorpe goes on for ever. He's quite unshockable, and I always knew that whatever happened I could go to Thorpe and he'd pick up the pieces. We leaned on him quite unashamedly. Still do, as you've seen.'

It must be nice to be able to lean on someone, Morag thought, made unusually wistful by the unpleasant little scene which had shaken her nerve more than she cared to think. Perhaps it was no wonder he behaved like an autocrat if his family came running to him for help any time things went wrong. But he had no right to treat her as though she was a none too honest kitchenmaid of the Victorian era. A kitchenmaid, moreover, with an eye to her employer's teaspoons!

Outside the darkness had lifted, driven by a crimson

dawn which subdued the moon into pallor in the western sky. From the trees behind the house a thrush sang a beautiful hymn to the new day, while a black-bird tugged at a worm in the lawn, its beak gold against the green of the grass. The tall yellow and orange clubs of the torch lilies moved and swayed when a tui plundered the flowers for nectar; as if in thanksgiving he perched on the top of one, lifted his white-banded throat to expose the bobble of feathers there and acted as chorus to the thrush, the bell-like notes blending with the thrush's shriller singing.

The homely beauty of it all caught at Morag's throat. Rapidly increasing light made the flowers in the border gleam. It might be the depths of winter, but here there were always flowers—the golds and reds of the day lilies, daisy bushes in their finery of yellow and pink and white, the froth of alyssum and the clear jewel colours of anemones and ranunculus. Jonquils gleamed golden and white, their scent lying freshly sweet over the garden, and beneath the trees in the orchard the earliest daffodils nodded in the thin pale rays of the sun.

'It always grabs me by the throat,' came Sally's voice from just behind.

Morag turned, her eyes glittering with a sheen which could not be tears. 'I'd forgotten,' she said huskily. 'Here, you shouldn't be out of bed without a robe.'

'It's warm enough.' Sally turned the now very sleepy Rachel towards the window. 'There you are, sweetie. If it stays fine you'll be able to kick in the sun on the terrace. You'll like that, won't you?'

It did stay fine, and Rachel lay in the old perambulator which had been dragged triumphantly down from the attic by Soldier, trying to catch the sun's rays in her chubby starfish hands while her elders reclined in deckchairs and watched the two boys construct a massive sandcastle.

'I'm glad Thorpe didn't alter things,' Sally said warmly. 'The boys love the sandpit and the swings, and when Graham and Louise have children they'll be here for them. Thorpe's too, though he doesn't seem to be very interested in perpetuating his genes.'

Her voice trailed away into silence. Morag looked across, thinking she had drifted off, but Sally's eyes, a paler green-blue than her brother's, were wide open and fixed on Morag with what seemed speculative interest. It might have been a trick of the light, however, for almost immediately the other girl grinned.

'You look a bit startled. Does the idea of Thorpe as a father surprise you? You know, I rather get the feeling that you don't like him overmuch.'

Unfortunately Sally was every bit as quick on the uptake as her brother. Morag knew that it would be quite hopeless to deny her dislike. So she said dryly, 'Well, he is a bit overpowering.'

'I know what you mean, but most women go crazy about him. I used to be the most popular girl at school because everyone hoped I'd invite them home for the hols. Poor old Thorpe! He's been chased until he's an expert in self-defence and counter-attack. I used to wonder if he'd ever been in love or if he'd never had the chance.' She paused as if inviting comment, but Morag didn't want to hear about Thorpe Cunningham and used the moment to call a warning to Jason who looked to be contemplating the use of his truck as a club on Richie's head.

It appeared, however, that Sally was obstinately determined to stick to the subject.

'I used to think that he'd got that hunted feeling too deeply ingrained in him to ever lower his guard enough to fall in love, but I think perhaps he has. Something he said once.' She paused, then said sadly, 'I don't think it was a happy affair. He said something about wanting yet hating, then quoted Shakespeare at me.'

Morag's expression must have mirrored her incredulous thoughts, for Sally gave a faint smile. 'He can quote quite a few famous authors. He's the brainy one of the family. And speaking of brains, I wonder what's got into Graham. He and Louise are remarkably tardy in coming to greet the prodigal sister.'

With a sigh of something that might have been irritation she reached down into her knitting bag, withdrawing the crimson pullover she was knitting for Jason. 'I could go over and see them, I suppose, seeing that they're only half a mile away, but I just can't summon up the energy. Morag, do you think I'll ever get over this wretched 'flu?'

'Probably,' Morag told her in cheerfully callous tones. 'Don't forget you're a nursing mother. That's a bit tiring, and with 'flu on top of it you'll take a little longer. You'll never get that pullover finished if you don't stop squinting at it as though it's a particularly loathsome reptile.'

'I hate knitting,' Sally sighed as she began. 'But if I say so myself I do it *beautifully*, and it's my one housewifely talent. I can't sew and I can't hang wallpaper, and the smell of paint makes me sick and I hate dirt under my fingernails, so we have a high school boy to do the gardens, and my cooking is only so-so. But when I look at my family neatly kitted out in my knitteds, I manage to overcome my crashing inferiority complex.'

Morag looked at the older girl with some surprise, realising that Sally really meant what she said. Somewhat thoughtfully she rose and separated the boys, now locked together in a life and death struggle on the remains of the sandcastle, soothing them with the promise of a walk out to the dog kennels.

'Have fun, my loves,' Sally called, softly, for Rachel looked as if she might sleep.

Morag turned the perambulator so that the baby was out of the sun, tucked a light rug over the chubby legs and was rewarded with a wide and charming smile. Then, a boy on each hand, she set off down the garden to where a small gate in a high hedge led into a different world.

So Sally felt the pangs of inadequacy just as other, less privileged mortals did. Somehow Morag had assumed that because she was a Cunningham her employer would have her brother's arrogant confidence. It was rather disconcerting to be proved wrong. Still, there could be no doubt of Thorpe's complete self-assurance. It would not do to let Sally's confidences lower her guard at all.

Beyond the hedge was the kitchen garden, neat and symmetrical with rows of herbs and vegetables, and then through another gate the gravelled track which led down the hill to the outbuildings, the woolshed and haybarn, the drafting pens and implement shed and an assortment of other buildings of various ages and sizes, all painted dull green, all sheltered by a wide band of trees. The business part of Wharuaroa.

The dogs lived in their own alley, each chained to its kennel at night. As it was day, there were only one or two left there, but the boys were rather grateful for this. One was a huntaway, a dog who barked sheep from place to place, and both twins had drawn closer to Morag the nearer they got to the kennels.

However, in spite of his deep rough bark he was friendly enough, and after a few seconds spent eyeing his rapidly wagging tail the boys patted his hairy intelligent head without too much coaxing.

'He looks angry,' Jason confided after a moment, 'but he's nice, Morag.'

'Most of them are.' She grinned down at him, then looked up as a Landrover came hurtling along the track to stop with a quite unnecessary jerk in front of one of the sheds. The driver flung out and into the shed, to return a few minutes later with some sort of tool.

'That's mine uncle!' exclaimed Richie, after a moment, his expression alert as he shaded his eyes with one hand.

The clear high voice travelled on the still air, for Graham turned and waved, then came across to where they waited.

Morag found an odd sense of disappointment deep within her. Perhaps she had carried an image of her first love around with her all of these years; if so, she owned ruefully, it had been sadly at fault. The Graham she remembered was young and eager with laughter in his eyes, not this stranger with a shuttered, wary expression and deep lines giving an air of petulance to his features.

'Hullo, kids,' he said off-handedly. 'Have a good trip up?'

The children stared at him, then Jason offered, 'We flew up on a plane.'

'Yes, I know.' He was obviously not interested, his blue gaze fixed on Morag's face. 'Long time no see,' he said without emphasis.

She smiled. 'A very long time. How are things?'

'Oh, fine. How's life for you?'

'Fine.'

And that was all. He nodded at the children, pro-

mised to come over to see them some time and said
goodbye, running back to the 'Rover as if he couldn't
wait to be gone.

Morag smiled, aware that one of life's gentler ironies
was the question, 'Whatever did I see in him?' Or 'her'
as the case might be. In her reminiscences he was a kind
of Prince Charming figure remembered with affection
because he had loved her and she had not felt more
than regard for him. And now he was nothing more
than a rather tense, nervy young man, too busy to make
any effort to please his nephews.

So much for any fears Thorpe might have had. It was
quite clear that he felt as much interested in Morag as
she felt in him. And speak of the devil. . . . Thorpe was
talking to Sally when they arrived back, or rather,
laughing with her.

It was the first time Morag had ever seen him when
he wasn't in a towering rage or keeping tight control
of himself, and she had to own with the greatest reluctance that he had more than his fair share of masculine sex appeal, if that was what you could call a kind
of intense virility which made any other man seem
pale and washed out by comparison. It wasn't just the
fact that his features were good, or that he was a big,
lithe man, she thought dispassionately. There were
plenty of handsome men around, and plenty of big
ones, but very few had that kind of inner strength
which made them immediately dominant in any
gathering.

He looked up as they came across the grass, and she
felt a return of that impotent anger which had assailed
her when he had waylaid her outside Sally's door. She
hated the appraisal he seemed to be making of her all
the time.

'We saw Uncle Graham,' Richie informed his mother. 'He was in a hurry.'

'Where was he?' Thorpe demanded, censure plain in his voice, his cold glance stabbing Morag's face.

'By the dogs.' Richie was surprised and a little frightened at his uncle's reaction.

Morag said levelly, 'He came tearing up in a Land-rover to get some tools.'

'I see.' Thorpe shrugged, perhaps aware that his sister was regarding him with some puzzlement. 'Something must have gone wrong with the 'dozer. He's putting in a dam over Pile's hill.'

Sally nodded. 'How did you like the dogs, boys?'

'Neat!' All fears forgotten, they boasted of their bravery, talking, as they often did, together, one beginning a sentence, the other finishing.

Morag went across to see if Rachel was still asleep. Fortunately, once she got off she was practically impossible to waken. Completely relaxed, she lay with one starfish hand outstretched, the other tucked under her cheek in a miniature imitation of Sally's usual sleeping position. Morag's heart contracted. She looked up, met Thorpe's level regard and flushed, oddly ill at ease. Anger lit small flames deep within her eyes. He had no right to—to *stare* at her so openly, she thought uncomfortably, aware that somehow she reacted with uncharacteristic tension to his glance. It was, of course, unpleasant to be the object of his dislike and contempt, but heavens, who cared what he thought of her!

Squaring her shoulders, she gave him back a cool level stare, only to feel heat once more along her cheekbones. Drat the man! With what came perilously near to a flounce she turned away, but it was some minutes before she regained enough composure to join in the conversation once more.

Already Sally seemed to have recovered some of her natural high spirits.

'The air,' she said, when Morag commented on it. 'And the glorious relief of knowing that big brother is in charge again! I'm afraid I'm not in the least independent, Morag. Not like you, for example.'

Morag shrugged. It was after lunch and the children were all asleep, exhausted from the morning's exercise, so she was curled up in the window seat of the room Sally called the parlour, gazing dreamily out on to the terrace.

'Independence is all very well,' she said drily. 'Sometimes I think I'd give anything for a shoulder to lean on.'

'Truly?' Sally looked her astonishment. 'You seem to be far too calm and confident and super-efficient to allow yourself that sort of weakness.'

'Oh, come on! A strong silent tower of strength would be absolutely marvellous when I'm tired. Mind you,' she added thoughtfully, 'I'd hate to *live* with anyone like that.'

'Me too. My Sandy is anything but. He talks all the time and panics madly, but I must rely on him far more than I thought. Very salutary, this desertion has been. I wonder how he's finding Antarctica.'

'Cold,' said Morag, and chuckled at the older girl's comical expression of disgust.

They must have seemed far more friendly than employer and nurse had any right to be, for the woman who came through the door looked with some bewilderment at Morag before saying, 'Hazel told me you had your nanny in here, Sally.'

'She's a Karitane nurse, Louise.' Sally performed the introductions, winked conspiratorially at Morag from behind her sister-in-law's back, and went on, 'And please don't upset her in any way, shape or form! If she leaves, I'll give you one of the brats to care for.'

'A dire threat,' Graham's wife said coolly, favouring Morag with a direct, level inspection. 'Thorpe said you used to live here in the valley, Miss Nelson.'

'Yes.'

Apparently Thorpe hadn't revealed anything else, for there was no consciousness in Louise's regard. Feeling rather as though she had been put in a false position, Morag replied politely to the woman's polite conversation, then chose what she thought was an appropriate time to stand up and make her departure.

But Sally said almost pleadingly, 'Don't go, Morag; you'll only find some work to do if you leave, and you need a few hours' rest each day!'

Which put Morag in an extremely awkward position, as Louise Cunningham's beautifully shaped brows lifted to express her surprise. Still, Sally was her employer, and as for reason Sally didn't want to be left alone with the beautiful Louise, it was up to Morag to do as she was asked.

Graham's wife was palely blonde, wide-eyed and possessing that skin which seems to grace only English beauties, clear and fine and soft. A tall, willowy woman, she made Morag feel frowsily short and awkward as well as out of place. It was, she thought, unfair of Sally to use her as buffer, but she was by now reconciled to such small foibles on the part of employers!

Nevertheless, a stilted twenty minutes followed until a noise floating down from overhead revealed that one at least of the children was awake. Grateful Morag left them and wondered as she climbed the stairs just what Graham had seen in his wife. She resembled an ice maiden, very cold, very self-possessed, not very interesting.

Not, she thought cheerfully, as she allowed Jason to dress himself, that she cared in the least. Louise Cunningham might feel that a Karitane nurse was a servant and had therefore no right to be in the parlour, but it wasn't going to affect said Karitane nurse one bit!

Sally was contrite but evasive when it came to explaining her actions.

'She's a bore,' she said, then with a thread of defiance, 'At least, not a bore, but *so* critical! And a bit of a snob. I was angry, so I used you. I'm sorry.' She seemed relieved to change the subject. 'You are coming down tonight, aren't you? Gray and Louise will be there, but you needn't mind them.'

Morag was quite adamant, however. 'No, I'll stay up. The children still aren't entirely at home here.'

'Oh dear. I'd hoped you'd give me some moral support. Gray and Thorpe are prickly at the best of times —at least, Gray is. Thorpe doesn't seem to care, but of course he knows he can crack the whip whenever he wants and Gray will jump. And dear Louise will sit there obviously regretting the fact that she married the younger brother.'

Morag shook her head at her. 'You're being indiscreet!'

'Oh, I know you won't chatter to others.' Petulantly Sally straightened a book on the table beside her chair, her movements nervous and jerky. 'You're the sort who's so discreet that wild horses wouldn't drag gossip from you. I like to talk. But quite frankly, Louise unnerves me. Gray has always had it for Thorpe; envy, I think, poor old dear, but until he married her he and Thorpe used to rub along reasonably well. Now, I think she's got Gray so strung up that he hates Thorpe. She wants Thorpe to give Gray half Wharuaroa, but of course Thorpe won't cut the station up. And Gray won't leave. He loves the place.'

'You shouldn't be telling me all this,' Morag said quietly, feeling an immense reluctance to hear any more about the Cunninghams. She wanted to remain completely detached from them, do her job then go away and never give them another thought; but Sally's confidences were making it impossible for her to view them in such an impersonal light. It irritated her that she should feel sorry for Graham, irritated her even more that she should be intensely aware of Thorpe Cunningham's presence in the house, so that she felt she should tiptoe around in case he noticed her.

Damn the man, she thought in frustration, having just found herself holding her breath as she walked down the hall past his study. He had no right to impinge on her awareness so strongly! Presence was all very well, but this was absolutely ridiculous. It seemed that the years were being stripped away from her and with them the defences she had built up so carefully, so that at Wharuaroa she was an eternal, naïve seventeen-year-old.

Fortunately she saw very little of him, for he rose at some ungodly hour and was gone from the house by the time she brought the children down.

As she ate with them in the kitchen she did not meet him at mealtimes. Dinner would have been the exception, but he was out for several nights running, so she was freed from his inimical presence even then.

Sally enjoyed her convalescence, resting in the sun and regaining her habitual cheerfulness, but little of her energy; the children responded equally well to Hazel's spoiling and Morag's discipline and slept like logs each night after wearing themselves out during the day.

On occasions Morag had to prevent herself from assuming that it was spring and not the depths of winter, the weather was so lovely. Everything conspired to trick the season. There were lambs in the paddocks, the house cow presented them with a long-legged gawky calf and the big red Hereford cows nuzzled their white-faced, blunt-headed offspring with bovine devotion.

Even the flowers were spring-like. Any minute now freesias would begin to bloom, and the daffodils and jonquils were still gay exclamations of gold in the garden. Soldier brought in orchids, and put them in jardinieres around the house, huge pots of the exotic things with their strap leaves and long arching stems of delicately poised blooms in all shades of gold and green, white and pink. Their faint scent mingled with that of the Japanese honeysuckle to form a sweetness in the air which permeated every corner of the house, making it springlike on even the greyest day. And every day she and the children picked a big bunch of Parma violets from the patch under the pepper tree and took them to Sally.

Much against her will Morag found herself falling in love with the homestead. It was, she thought wryly, a gracious place, unlike the people who lived there. At least, for 'the people' read 'that person!'

Impatiently she shook her head. He was too much in her thoughts these days, and she did not like it, aware that that way lay danger. Physical attraction could be devastating if it wasn't firmly scotched, and she was knowledgeable enough to realise that if she was not very firm with herself she could join the queue of all the other women who had found Thorpe's masculine arrogance very attractive. No man should have his splendid physical presence as well as that kind of steel-hard strength which appealed to even the most liberated of women; it seemed distinctly unfair.

Morag disliked him, and yet without even trying she could see him in her mind's eye as clearly as if he were before her, the deceptively lazy stride, the suggestion of power in shoulders and arms, strongly chiselled features redeemed from conventional good looks by the purposefulness in them.

Stop it! she scolded herself. You're behaving like a fool! But as she tackled the pile of ironing she was doing, she could not banish him from her mind, and when he walked into the room she was not particularly surprised, although her heart did a funny jump in her breast.

Without preamble he demanded furiously, 'Why did you tell Louise that you and Graham had been lovers?'

Morag kept her astounded glance lowered, folding Richie's shirt carefully before replying as coolly as she could, 'I haven't. And we weren't.'

Perhaps the lack of protest, or perhaps the flat conviction of her voice convinced him. A glance as bright and sharp as a stiletto held her eyes for a moment, then he nodded, pushing his hand across the back of his neck as though it hurt.

'Then I suppose Gray did,' he said tonelessly. 'The *bloody* fool!'

Morag couldn't think of any reply to this, so she applied herself to her ironing, but after a moment she asked, 'Does your neck hurt?'

'What? Oh, no. A habit I have, apparently.' He viewed her with a kind of grim displeasure before leaning back against the wall of the ironing room. 'I said you were a catalyst, didn't I,' he remarked in tones which were almost conversational. 'And don't tell me you've done nothing, I know that. Just looked demure and efficient and the tiniest bit smug. Only your presence here has caused an almighty disruption between Graham and Louise. Does that please you?'

Morag lifted her lashes to meet his hard scrutiny. Without emphasis she said, 'I can assure you that it doesn't please me in the least. And I can also assure you that Graham and I were *never* lovers!'

'Naturally,' he said curtly. 'I don't expect you to change your story now.'

'Will you *listen*?' she exploded, the hot colour giving sudden drama to her features. 'I was not——'

'Shut up!'

He jerked his head towards the window, wide open to let in the sweet air. Frozen by his peremptory command, Morag listened, to hear voices rising and falling not too far away.

'I was *not* Graham's mistress,' she finished more softly but every bit as firmly. It was very important to convince him of this, but one look at his countenance made it quite obvious that he didn't believe a word she was saying.

A faint, contemptuous smile touched his lips.

'Oddly enough, I'd think more of you if you admitted it,' he said after a moment, 'but I gather your pride is important to you. I don't care about that aspect of it; all that concerns me is that Louise is just about hysterical because she believes that you and Graham have taken up where you left off.'

'*Oh!*' Morag breathed out the syllable so furiously that the hand holding the iron trembled and she had to set it down. To her extreme dismay her eyes filled with tears of rage and frustration, made all the more humiliating because a swift search in her pockets failed to produce a handkerchief, so she was forced to wipe her eyes with the back of her hand and give a most inelegant sniff.

'Don't cry *now*,' he exclaimed as if she had done it deliberately to annoy him. 'Here, for heaven's sake use this.'

'This' was a large handkerchief. Morag blew her nose with defiance and said thickly, 'She must be neurotic. She *must* know that we've met only the once. She must——'

'She *is* neurotic,' he agreed. 'She does know that you've met only once. She's everything you can think of. She also happens to be the love of Gray's life, God help him, and at the moment she's talking wildly of leaving him and going back home. And that will kill him.'

Morag stared, saw stark honesty in his face and with some care ironed Jason's denims for the second time.

Silence stretched between them and with it tension until at last, goaded into speech, Morag said ungraciously, 'Well, I suppose I'll have to go, then. Heaven knows I didn't want to make any trouble.'

'I doubt if you can help it,' he returned, a thread of sardonic humour warming the deep tones. 'You seem to have some strange effect on this family. As it happens, I doubt if your removal will help matters now. Louise is shatteringly possessive and very insecure. She's quite capable of convincing herself that he's seeing you behind her back.'

Before she could say anything which might be not only disrespectful but downright scathing, Morag pressed her lips firmly together.

'Wise girl.' Thorpe frowned, thinking deeply, then lifted an ironic brow at her. 'About the only thing that will allay her suspicions is an affair between you and me,' he observed calmly.

Morag's mouth opened in a soundless O as the betraying colour touched her cheeks and throat.

'Exactly,' he agreed, as though she had spoken. 'But you must bear at least some of the blame. No woman, however stable she is or isn't, would like the thought of one of her husband's old girl-friends turning up out of the blue.'

'Oh, no, you don't!' Morag retorted with spirit, refusing to allow herself to be browbeaten into accepting such a dangerous theory. 'You're not blaming me! Lord, people meet old girl-friends and boy-friends all the time. New Zealand is so small that you can't turn round without tripping over someone you worshipped at the age of sixteen. I refuse to admit fault!'

'At least admit that if it hadn't been for your arrival back here this wouldn't have happened.'

Caught, she hesitated, the angry flush dying away as her obtrusive and quite unnecessary conscience forced her to admit just that. 'I suppose so,' she said grudgingly, adding quickly, 'I've only your word for what did happen.'

'You can take it as accurate,' he told her coldly. 'Why on earth did you have to come back, Morag? I should have got rid of you the night you turned up with Sally.'

Stung by the bleak relentless note in his voice as much as by his words, she snapped, 'I wish I'd gone! The thing is, if you lot behaved like normal human beings, instead of refugees from a mental home, none of this would have happened.'

'Well, it has, and I'm very much afraid that we'll all have to take the consequences.' He startled her by switching the iron off at the wall, adding peremptorily, 'Stop using that as a shield! Why isn't Hazel doing this, anyway?'

'It's part of my job.' Nervous without the iron which she had, as he'd pointed out, been using as a shield against his forceful presence, she backed off, then realised that she was revealing by her actions just how he affected her. 'Look,' she argued desperately, 'wouldn't it be better if I left? I mean ...'

'Scared of me?' he asked mockingly, sounding devilishly assured.

Her temper flared. 'No, I'm not scared of you! I don't like the idea of pretending an emotion I don't feel, that's all. And I hate deceit. Sally will wonder what on earth is going on.'

He shrugged. 'I doubt it. She'll probably be rather pleased. She's been trying to marry me off for the past five years.'

'M-marry you——!' Morag's lashes flew up to meet the saturnine intensity of his gaze.

'Oh, don't worry,' he drawled. 'I don't intend to sacrifice my freedom for Graham's happiness. When you and Sally leave here our affair will fizzle out naturally, but by that time we should have been able to convince Louise that she need not fear for Graham.'

Morag pushed a hand through her hair, unable to hide the strain that sharpened her features. Thorpe looked calmly confident, but then there was a tiny muscle flickering in his jaw which warned her that he would stand no more argument, and she was afraid as she had never been before in her life. No doubt he was sophisticated enough to enjoy a flirtation in spite of his low opinion of her, but she knew that she wouldn't be able to cope with such a situation.

'Look——' she began, but the words died before they had even been formed, for he took her wrist and brought her up against him, something very like anger flaming into incandescence in the blue-green depths of his gaze.

'You don't find me horrible to touch,' he said calmly. 'It should be quite easy.'

He looked a moment longer into her dilated eyes before lowering his head. Morag, realising what he was about to do, moved convulsively, but he used his great strength to subdue her struggles and took his time about kissing her very thoroughly and with every appearance of enjoyment.

Unfortunately Morag enjoyed it too, if such a word could be used for a sensation which terrified the wits out of her. He did not make the mistake of forcing her, but his mouth was warm and tantalising, and when she relaxed in involuntary surrender he moved it to the pulse-beat in the hollow of her throat. For the first time in her life Morag felt desire shiver through her like a pain, and she trembled and tried to push him away.

'Calm down,' he said, his voice amused yet decisive. 'Anybody would think you'd never been kissed before.'

'Let me go! Of course I've been kissed, but not—not in cold blood. Thorpe ...' Her voice trailed off as he lifted his head and she met his eyes and saw there desire which was as fierce as it was impersonal.

'I'm sorry,' he said with sardonic emphasis. 'Perhaps this is more to your liking?'

It was an assault on her senses, a kiss without respect or consideration, hard, demanding and as sensual as if he had bought her for the night and was determined to get his money's worth. Morag felt the blood drum in her ears and when his hand moved to pull her body against the hardness of his she kicked his shin viciously and twisted away, her breath coming in short gasps between her bruised lips, as she confronted him from behind the relative safety of the ironing board.

'You touch me again,' she threatened, speaking softly, because the voices outside the window seemed to be coming closer, 'and I'll pack up and go. As a matter of fact, I think I'll go anyway.'

He leaned back against the wall, all trace of the passion which had so frightened her gone, once more completely in control of himself and the situation. Not that he had ever lost control, Morag thought wildly. She had been the one who had felt her sanity slip away from her at the unleashed response of her body to his, and she despised herself for it.

'If you leave her,' he said calmly, 'I'll make sure that you never get another job in this country.'

'You threatened me with that before, but you couldn't do it.'

'Oh, yes, I could!'

She stared at him with hostile fury, meeting the implacable steadiness of his glance, and knew that—somehow—he would do it.

Her breath came slowly in a long sigh as she capitulated.

'I don't believe you, but I'll stay. Only because I don't want to leave Sally in the lurch. And because I was fond of Graham, once.'

'You'll stay because I say you stay,' he said coolly, refusing to accept her face-saving words.

Morag shook her head. 'And on my terms.'

Sudden amusement warmed the cold depths of his eyes. 'I'll admit you've got guts. O.K. What are these terms?'

'I'm not your plaything,' she said shortly, hardening her heart against the very masculine appeal he exerted when he was amused. The arrogance was always there, of course, but the fact that he had a sense of humour made him seem more human, less the cold autocrat.

'And what exactly is that supposed to mean?'

'You know perfectly well. I don't want any more on-slaughts like the one you just inflicted on me.'

His smile was slow and saturnine, very assured. 'Have it your own way, but for a few seconds you enjoyed that onslaught, as you call it, until your Aunt Kate's train-ing came to the fore.' Straightening up, he became curt and businesslike. 'Very well, I'll try to keep my raging lust within bounds, provided you stop being provoca-tive. All I ask is that you respond in kind to any over-tures I make in public. And remember—Louise is an astute woman.'

CHAPTER THREE

EVEN then Morag almost convinced herself that it was
all a storm in a teacup, that no woman could be as
neurotic as the Louise that Thorpe had described. If
she had not met the woman later that afternoon she
might have refused to have anything more to do with
Thorpe's scheme. But it took only one searing, suspicious glance from Graham's wife to convince her that
the woman did indeed suspect the worst.

And perhaps Morag might have taken the other
alternative and left Wharuaroa, risking Thorpe's displeasure, if Sally hadn't decided that she was too tired
to go down to dinner that night.

'You go down,' she said from the chaise-longue
in her room. 'I'll leave the door open and if any of the
children squeak I'll see to them. You haven't had a day
off since you came to us, thanks to my wretched 'flu, so
at least enjoy this evening!'

Morag hesitated, frowning at the pale fragility of her
employer's features. 'Very well, but only if you promise
me that you'll go to the doctor tomorrow and get him
to check you over.'

'You drive a hard bargain, but for you, anything.'
Sally smiled and drew a rug over her legs. 'Go on, put
something pretty on and startle Thorpe! I have a
notion my big brother finds you intriguing.'

The faint flush that warmed Morag's cheeks made
the other woman chuckle knowingly, but fortunately
for her nurse's peace of mind she did not pursue the
subject. Morag was able to escape, bitterly cursing a

treacherous skin which revealed her embarrassment
only too readily.

When she came downstairs after seeing the children
asleep and Sally tucked up in bed with a bloodcurdling
thriller and a bowl of delicious-smelling chicken broth
prepared by a rather anxious Hazel, it was to find that
she and Thorpe were alone in the big drawing room.
Almost she fled back up the stairs, but he turned to
greet her when she arrived at the door and there was
no escape.

'How is Sally?' he asked, after he had given her
sherry.

'A bit frail.' Morag paused before asking, 'Was she
always as delicate as this?'

'I think so. I can remember my mother giving her
an evil-tasting tonic every winter.' He smiled and the
unfair charm became blatant. 'I remember her tantrums about it, too. She used to scream to lift the roof!'

Morag smiled, but it must have seemed abstracted,
because after a moment he asked, 'Are you worried?'

'No, not really. She's promised to go to the doctor
tomorrow, anyway.'

'Ah yes. Sarah Griffiths has known her since she was
a baby, so she'll be able to allay your fears.' He touched
a cord which pulled the curtains together and said,
'Come closer to the fire. You look cold. Or perhaps it's
the dress.'

Morag stiffened, regarding him with acute dislike.
The dress was one of her restrained ones, a cool pale
green wool jersey which was neat but not startling, and
she did not need a reminder of the fact that it did little
for her colouring.

'Anybody,' he continued, smiling at her narrowly,
'would be excused for thinking that you made very
little effort to look attractive this evening. You showed

a better taste in clothes when you were seventeen.'

'As you remember,' she scoffed, seating herself with prim movements in an upright carved chair which was distinctly French in flavour, as were all of the fittings in this lovely formal room.

'Oh, I remember.' And at the open disbelief she showed he grinned unkindly and listed, 'Several pairs of skin-tight jeans, three or four pairs of shorts, denim too, and an assortment of brief, clinging tops mostly in shades of pink and gold which did a lot more for you than that outfit.'

Uncertainly she returned, 'You must have a remarkable memory.'

'Incredible,' he said drily. 'You caused me a vast amount of worry that year, which is probably why I remember so well. And of course, everywhere I went I seemed to fall over you.'

'None of my doing, I assure you,' she retorted swiftly, feeling distinctly ill at ease. His assumption that she and Graham had been lovers made her angry yet cautious. His belief smirched the memory of that innocent little childish affair so that wariness tightened her nerves when he referred to it.

'I believe you. You had eyes only for Graham.'

He half-turned away to pour himself a drink. From beneath lowered lashes Morag noted the broad sweep of his shoulders and the quiet smooth grace of his movements. She felt an odd jerk in the pit of her stomach and to banish it sipped at her sherry, wishing half-heartedly that she smoked. It would be useful to hide behind a smoke-screen, especially when Thorpe was surveying her with those eyes which saw too much. On the verge of reminding him that six years ago he had told her that she did not love Graham she hesitated, then stopped. Some deep reluctance held her back. The episode was over and the sooner forgotten the better.

'Just one thing,' he said, lifting his glass to her in a mock salute. 'How did you explain to your aunt where you'd got the money to keep you while you were training?'

Morag shrugged, her distaste clear. 'I didn't. I just wrote them a note when I left. She didn't care much, poor Aunt Kate. I think they were probably glad to see the back of me.'

'They were hardly suitable guardians for any child,' he commented without much expression. 'Do you enjoy your work?'

'Oh yes!'

As the evening wore on Morag discovered to her surprise that when he cared to be he was an interesting and entertaining host and oddly easy to talk to. Slowly, under the influence of his impersonal charm she relaxed and told him of some of the highlights of her life as a Karitane nurse, drawing laughter from him on several occasions.

After the superbly cooked dinner she ran up to see Sally, already halfway through her thriller and most reluctant to leave it, then made her way back down the stairs, wary at spending the rest of the evening exposed to the formidable Cunningham charm yet unable to avoid an excited anticipation which warned her of the danger she was in.

Not that he made any move towards her at all. As she prepared for bed Morag realised that he had behaved as if that kiss had never happened.

Company manners, she told herself sternly, and wondered why she felt almost cheated. Surely she had not hoped for anything more than politeness?

It shamed her to have to admit that whatever was

between them was growing in strength rather than fading, and the more she saw of him the harder it was going to be to fight his potent attraction, especially in the situation Louise's obsessive jealousy had forced on them.

Most of all it was infuriating to realise that his opinion meant so much to her. Never before had she been dependent on a man's good opinion. Fiercely she told herself that she would not allow herself to be put in a position where her emotions were jeopardised just to satisfy the neurotic fancies of a jealous woman.

A restless night convinced her that the only sensible thing to do was to put as much distance between her and Thorpe Cunningham as she possibly could. After all, it was not as though Sally needed her any longer, she thought, slamming the door on her conscience; surely she and Hazel could cope with the children.

But when Thorpe brought his sister back from the doctor's the following day he looked grim and Sally, in spite of a brave attempt at cheerfulness, went straight to bed. Morag brought the baby in to her and it was easy to see that she had been crying, but as she said nothing Morag did not ask, her own personal worries swamped by Sally's.

After lunch the children slept and Thorpe chose this time to ask Morag if she would come into the small sitting-room.

Once there he said abruptly, 'You're too astute not to see that something is wrong.'

There was no answer to this, but Morag nodded, her brows contracting into a frown as she met the level blue-green of his glance and saw that something had thrown him well off balance.

'Dr Griffiths isn't sure, but she thinks there could be something wrong with Sally's heart.'

'Oh *no*!'

'Yes; she has to have tests, of course, but Sarah thinks there could be a weakness in the valves.'

Moved by compassion, Morag put her hand on his arm, saying seriously, 'There's so much they can do now, Thorpe.'

'I know.' He looked down at her fingers, pale but practical with the shiny nails of perfect health.

Rebuffed by the chill intensity of his regard, Morag went to move back. Obviously she had overstepped the invisible mark he had set between them.

But he covered her hand with his and smiled rather crookedly. 'Trying to comfort me, Morag, like a good little nurse? Thanks, but it's not necessary. I know what it entails—so does Sally. Sarah believes in full explanations.' He dropped his hand and frowned, becoming once more the hard-headed employer. 'She'll need you now more than ever. I want your promise that you won't leave her in the lurch.'

Morag snatched her hand back as if the touch of his arm poisoned her. 'You know,' she said with a glittering smile, 'if you spent your time thinking up ways to be nasty you couldn't be more successful. Or is your opinion of me so low that you assume that I'd take off at a time like this?'

'Don't be a fool,' he snapped. 'And give me credit for some sense as well. I know you've found yourself in a situation you don't like. I wouldn't blame you for wanting to get away, so my opinion of you doesn't come into it at all. I want your promise.'

'You have it,' she said shortly, angry now with herself for giving him the opportunity to point out how little she meant to him.

'Thank you.'

The forbidding courtesy repelled her, as no doubt it

was meant to. Without further thought she snapped, 'Think nothing of it!'

He let her get to the door, then said without expression, 'By the way, Graham and Louise will be here for dinner. I want you there—and not in that thing you had on last night. If we're to convince Louise that I find you—interesting you're going to have to wear something a little more alluring.'

'I don't wear alluring clothes.'

He lifted his brows in mocking query. 'Oh, come now, Morag. I don't believe that!' Again that slow measuring glance which seemed to leave her naked.

The bold insolence of it brought an answering flush to her cheeks, but her eyes were steady and slightly contemptuous. 'Credit *me* with some sense,' she returned in mockery of his words to her a few moments ago.

'Sense—or calculation?'

'Self-preservation.'

For some reason he looked angry at that, but after a moment the broad shoulders lifted in the slightest of shrugs. 'It doesn't matter. Just wear something reasonable. You don't have to look like a film star, but I'm not normally attracted to dowdy nonentities.'

'I'll do my best,' she returned coldly before putting an end to the interview by marching through the door without a backward glance.

Infuriating autocrat! she fumed as she climbed the stairs. He had the cheek of Attila the Hun—and oh, wouldn't she just love to cut him down to size! Of all the gall! Groping for more adjectives to describe him, she gave up in disgust, and contemplated the fact that she should get so angry with him and yet not be immune to the strong sexual attraction he possessed. It was normal enough, of course. Attraction was a physical thing, a desire of the eyes and glands, and it didn't really matter much what character the desired one possessed. It seemed a pity that she had to feel it for someone like Thorpe Cunningham who was not too scrupulous about using the advantage his superb physical presence gave him.

Morag had thought herself in love several times, discovering her mistakes fairly soon. Nobody could call her experienced, she thought gloomily as she folded the baby's clothes, but she had acquired enough sophistication to recognise masculine interest when it focussed on her. If she showed herself willing Thorpe would flirt with her, probably indulge in a little mild lovemaking. If she showed even more willing he might attempt a seduction, but she thought not. Well aware of his effect on women, he yet had an aura of self-control which seemed to be stronger through constant use, and he was the sort of man who would consider it beneath his dignity to have an affair with an employee. Or anyone under his roof, if it came to that, she concluded, and couldn't help wondering just how she would react if he did try to make love to her. She had a horrid feeling that her resistance would be a token one. Thorpe Cunningham didn't look just experienced; she was prepared to bet her bottom dollar that he had been born with the knowledge of how to dazzle women into submission. No doubt his technique had become refined over the years, but his knowledge was instinctive.

And really, a man with his kind of looks and that air of masculine authority backed by a keen intelligence didn't need much more than that to interest women. The rest, that lithe grace and the sensual awareness, were bonuses. He was, Morag decided, altogether too well endowed by the Fates. No doubt, in time, he would marry some equally well endowed woman who would give him children and run his household satisfactorily and play lady of the manor. It seemed that that was all he would expect of a wife. Except, of course, for a reciprocal passion to meet his. Thorpe was entirely too self-sufficient to submit to the agonies and anguishes of love, the rare intimacy which marks it from its lesser brother lust. Not for him the desire to lose himself entirely in the beloved, in an ecstasy of giving without counting the cost.

A fact which she had better not forget, she told herself, frowning ferociously at one of Rachel's nightgowns. Desire was one thing; he could supply that. Love was entirely another, and it was highly unlikely that he would ever allow himself to love, so it would be quite useless for anyone, especially Morag Nelson, to get ideas about that!

Fortunately Dr Griffiths had laid down no strict regimen for her patient, beyond telling her that on no account was she to overdo herself.

'Which is just as well,' Sally told Morag as they watched the boys in the sandpit from the loungers on the terrace. 'She knows that I'd go mad if I had to stay in bed, or anything like that.'

'When do you go for your tests?'

'Dr Griffiths will ring and let me know. I must say I'm a bit jittery, but she said that valve ops are almost routine now, so I'm not going to get in a tizz.'

'What about your husband?'

Sally looked mutinous, folding her mouth into a firm line.

'Thorpe wants to tell him—we could contact him by radio. But I won't have it. He's snowed in down there and there's no way he can get out until spring, so that all telling him would do would be to make him worry unnecessarily. With any luck he'll emerge from his igloo or whatever they live in at Scott Base and find it's all over.'

'He has a right to know,' said Thorpe, walking through the doors of the little parlour behind them. 'Don't you agree, Morag?'

A delicate flush touched her cheekbones at this casual use of her Christian name, but she said with spirit, 'I refuse to become embroiled in an argument. Just one thing, though, Sally. If by some remote chance things do go wrong——'

'I've thought about that too,' Sally interrupted, displaying such determination that for a moment she looked very much like her brother. 'And I still think I'm right. Thorpe, you must promise not to go behind my back.'

He regarded her with some astonishment, then said in a gentler voice than Morag had ever heard him use, 'O.K.', if it means that much to you. On one condition, however.'

'Always you have a condition,' said Sally, half laughing, half serious. 'Very well then, give.'

'That you stay here until he comes back.'

In spite of herself Morag's glance flew to meet his, saw it hard and diamond-sharp. When Sally laughed and agreed she could have wept, for it meant that she was doomed to spend her time in close proximity to him until—when on earth did the pack ice break up in Antarctica? That was when conditions became suitable for flying once more. She had a feeling that it was in November, which meant that she was stuck here for at least three months!

Her dismayed glance met the sardonic amusement of his; chagrined, she bit her lip, turning her head to avoid that scrutiny while she scolded herself for her transparency. Thorpe was just the cynic to be amused by the fact that her attraction to him was as reluctant as it must be obvious.

Muttering something, she jumped up and went across to the twins, now joining forces to build an edifice higher than either of them. They greeted her with restrained enthusiasm, warning her that they wanted no help.

She stayed for a few moments admiring their effort, before moving across the close-clipped lawn to where a camellia tree flaunted its huge coral blooms. A bee plundered pollen from the long golden stamens, then rose groggily into the shimmering air. It was deceptively warm for winter, but high in the blue sky a veil of clouds heralded a change. Tomorrow could bring rain or wind. Absently her fingers caressed the silken petals of a flower, touching the smoothness with loving sympathy.

She felt his presence before his hand twisted the flower from the branch and tucked it behind her ear and he stood smiling down into her startled face with cool irony.

'It suits you,' he said. 'Which is the correct ear?'

'I don't know,' she retorted, confused by his nearness and her body's reaction to it. Ignoring the nervous fluttering of her nerves, she continued desperately, 'Isn't it that you have a man if it's behind your right ear? But it should be a hibiscus flower.'

'Have you ever been to the Islands?'

'No. Have you?'

Stupid question, for of course he had. He had been everywhere.

'Yes, I liked them very much. Would you like to come into Kerikeri with me?'

Almost she gaped, her glance leaving his face to move to Sally, who grinned and nodded her head.

'She's given her permission,' he said smoothly. 'And I won't take no for an answer.'

'I believe you,' Morag retorted drily. 'But I can't leave Sally to cope with the boys.'

'Rubbish.' He took her hand and drew her across to the terrace. 'She's got a conscience,' he told his sister.

'Don't be silly, Morag. You haven't had any time off for weeks, so go with him. Hazel and I can cope. Buy some souvenirs or something while Thorpe does whatever he has to. Or just have a look around to see what's changed.'

Morag smiled. If she objected any more Sally would think her coy; it was quite obvious that her employer wanted her to like Thorpe, wanted him to like her. Matchmaker, Morag thought with grim humour as she let herself be led away into the house. If only poor Sally knew!

The road down into Kerikeri was good, still gravelled, but a far cry from the potholed horror it had been when Morag lived at Wharuaroa. Thorpe apparently felt no need to keep up the masquerade when there were no onlookers, so she used the silence to look around.

After some miles she ventured, 'It looks much more tidy than it used to.'

'Increased prosperity.' He slanted her a sideways glance. 'In spite of what you hear from the media we've had good years recently, and with better communications the North is becoming more like the rest of New Zealand.'

'I liked it when it was wild,' she said, wistfulness colouring her tones. 'We used to see rabbits on this road. I remember a little black one ran across just about here.'

'We? You and Graham?'

She flushed, and was angry at herself for reacting to the harsh note in his voice. Really, she was behaving like a schoolgirl!

'Yes. He tried to hit it, I remember, and I got angry.' She produced her reminiscence defiantly, daring him to make something of it.

'You have a vivid memory,' he said with smooth insolence. 'Does it extend to the details of the day I gave you money to get rid of you?'

'Oh yes. I remember that *very* clearly.' Bitterness roughened her voice, brought a diamond hardness to the depths of her eyes. 'I don't think I'll ever forget it.'

'Engraved on your memory?' He sounded sarcastic, as though he was trying to hurt her. 'Just don't think that the same thing is likely to happen again. You have no claim on me.'

'If I'm such an unscrupulous adventuress,' she demanded furiously without giving herself time to think, 'aren't you afraid that I might seduce you and then demand recompense?'

He smiled, a movement of his lips quite without amusement, before saying arrogantly, 'You wouldn't have a chance, my dear. I could kiss you stupid and not feel a thing.'

The conversation had got definitely out of hand, but Morag was still too angry at his chauvinistic attitude to keep a guard on her tongue. Incredulously she exclaimed,

'My God, you're an arrogant brute! I hope I see the day when some woman brings you to your knees, then gives you a good hard kick!'

'Does it hurt to know that I'm immune to your charms?' he asked with a narrow smile. 'Just so that you don't ever think that you might be the woman.'

Morag stared at him, saw the cold derision in his expression and felt as she had felt when she was seventeen, helpless and humiliated before a mercilessly insensitive autocrat. Her fingers clenched white on her lap, then uncurled. With a return to her normal coolness she said, 'Believe me, Mr Cunningham, I wouldn't have you if you were offered me on a silver plate. It would take more than money and good looks to sweeten your total lack of humanity for me.'

There was a tense silence, a stretching of time when it seemed that he gathered himself for the spring. Morag's teeth clenched on her lip. She had been inexcusably rude to him; in spite of the provocation he had offered, she should have remembered her place and stayed silent. From beneath her lashes she sent a quick glance towards the ruthless line of his profile, saw him smile and shivered. Like a fool she had underestimated him, in spite of the power which made him stand out in any gathering. Beneath the sophisticated man of the world, competent and hardworking businessman, there was a Thorpe who was primitive and fierce, and she, with her quick temper, had flicked that male ego on the raw.

Resisting the sudden urge to press against the back of the seat and make herself as small as possible, she said stiffly, 'I had no right to say that. I'm sorry.'

He turned and looked at her, ice over fire, menace barely held in check. 'You almost made a challenge of it, Morag.'

'Oh no!' The dark mass of her hair gleamed as she shook her head. 'I'm not throwing any challenges your way.'

'Afraid?' The word was a taunt.

'Yes.' She said it quite coolly, lifting eyes which were detached and withdrawn behind the thick hedge of her lashes. 'I know your capacity for ruthlessness and I'm not up to dealing with it. I don't want trouble.'

'Is that the story of your life? You left Wharuaroa when it seemed I might make trouble, you wear clothes which conceal your body in colours which make your skin sallow and your eyes flat, you agree to a deception you find distasteful because I threaten you. Do you always run away from trouble, Morag, hide your head in the hope that it will go away?'

'You said it,' she said wearily.

'And yet you have the air of a fighter.'

'Fighter?' She laughed bitterly, staring down at her hands as they rested tensely in her lap. 'Fighting doesn't get you anywhere in this world. Not when the power rests in others. I discovered that when I went to the orphanage. Then I came here. I fought that too, but nothing happened. Graham offered me a way out, but I knew that he wanted me only to spite you. And you were the one with the power—you got rid of me without any effort at all.' She moved restlessly, old wounds thickening her voice with remembered pain, the tender curve of her cheek turned away from him. 'Oh, what's the use! You have no idea how it feels to be a puppet, forced to move when someone pulls the strings. I should never have come back.'

'Why did you?'

'Because there was no chance of Sally finding anyone to take my place.' Her lips compressed into a thin line. 'I asked, but had no joy. And I was fool enough to think that in six years everyone would have forgotten.'

'What an extraordinarily repressed creature you are,' he remarked with indolent interest. 'I think you sell yourself a little short, however. You did pay me back, and you came back in spite of the fact that you must have known there would be some unpleasantness.'

'I hoped not. However, we're taught that our first loyalty is to the children. So I had to come. As for the other——' She shrugged. 'I don't like feeling beholden to anyone. I took your cheque because I was furious with you. I was going to tear it up in front of you. Then I realised that it was about the only way I had of escaping.' She smiled without humour. 'Looking back, it all seems very melodramatic and childish. Why were you in such a tizz? You must have known that if left alone things would die a natural death. Both Graham and I were very young and immature.'

'Not too immature to sleep together,' he said with that disconcerting crudeness which so shocked her every time he employed it. Ignoring her muffled gasp, he continued, 'Things were very sticky and Graham was determined to marry you. I had the impression that if you found yourself pregnant you'd marry him as a refuge, in spite of the fact that I was damned sure you didn't even have a crush on him, let alone love him.'

'Did he tell you we were lovers?' she asked quietly.

'Yes. Not that he needed to. It was fairly obvious that he'd grown up overnight, and there was only one reason for that.'

He sounded curt, as if the subject was repugnant to him. Morag could understand his reactions. She had the feeling that he was a fastidious man and the idea of lovers, however young, forced to consummate their love furtively and in secret would seem sordid to him. As it did to her.

Aloud she said, 'I suppose it's no use to repeat that regardless of what he said we were not lovers?'

'No.' It was a flat denial, completely convinced. After a moment he went on, 'Oh, don't get the idea I blame you for it. God knows, you had no one to look after you or care for you, and I suppose an orphanage's moral teachings would consist of a long list of don'ts. I've no doubt that Graham was very persuasive, and if he promised marriage—well, you wouldn't be the first girl who found it hard to say no.' He turned his head, looking sideways at her with eyes which gleamed with some unrecognisable emotion. 'Believe me, I'm in no position to start throwing stones.'

The implication made her feel sick. Softly, with no expression, she said, 'I wonder why he said that. Probably to get his own way; he might have felt that if you thought he had an obligation to me you would have allowed the marriage. If so, he underestimated you. We weren't lovers, Thorpe.'

'As I said before, and on the same subject, I find the truth, however distasteful, preferable to lies,' he returned harshly. 'If your guilt forces you to lie about it then you need to do something about it.'

'Oh, leave it,' she said tiredly.

He seemed content enough to accept her suggestion, retiring into his former silence as Morag looked around. They had come over the line of hills which formed the watershed between the Bay of Islands and the interior and were now swooping down towards the basin around Kerikeri. A panorama of greens ranging from the dark blue-green of the bush to the vivid lime of the winter pastures spread itself before them. Kerikeri was embowered in its tufty groves of high eucalypts; beyond it were the glittering waters of the deeply indented Bay, the islands merging into the high, grape-blue hills of the southern headland behind Russell.

'Oh!' she exclaimed, shocked from silence by the sight of a Taiwan cherry in full cerise splendour. 'How lovely!'

'We tried the cherries from one of those, Graham and I, when we were very young.' Thorpe smiled, revealing the potent charm which made him so attractive when he wished it. 'They were as bitter as gall. It was years before I would try the eating cherries my mother used to have flown up from the South Island.'

'The first year I went south I gorged on cherries and apricots,' Morag answered, determined to meet his mood. 'I missed the tamarillos, though, and feijoas. And picking mandarins and tangelos off a tree in the back garden.'

They talked lightly of various things, their past animosity glossed over for the present, until the road ran down the hill between the bamboo hedges into Kerikeri.

Then Thorpe said, 'I'm going to see the solicitor, and I estimate I'll be there for an hour. Can you amuse yourself for that length of time?'

'Of course,' she replied a little distantly.

Kerikeri had grown, of course, and she knew very few of the faces in the street, but she spent an enjoyable time browsing through the craft shops and galleries which seemed to have found a very suitable environment there.

It was in one of these, while she was standing in front of an exhibition of local pottery, that she heard someone say breathlessly from behind, 'Excuse me . . .'

As the voice trailed away Morag turned, her smile immediately summoning an answering one to the face of the girl who was standing behind her.

'I knew it was you! You haven't changed a bit, except to look a lot sleeker and more expensive. Do you remember me, Morag?'

'How could I forget Lauren Vodanovich?' Morag laughed. 'The wickedest girl in the school!'

The girl opened her huge brown eyes wide. 'Lauren Ramsgate now—I've been married for a couple of years. What *are* you doing here, Morag? I didn't think you would ever come back.'

Morag shrugged, realising that she would have to tell this old school friend the circumstances of her return. Lauren had not known very much of what had happened six years ago, for Morag was a reserved girl even then, but she knew enough about it to make an obvious effort to subdue her curiosity at the end of the explanation. For which Morag was grateful.

'You'll have to come and see us on one of your days off,' Lauren said hospitably. 'Hazel knows where we live, and I'd love to show you my house.'

'I'd like that.' If she was bound to stay at Wharuaroa until the weather in Antarctica permitted Sandy Johnston to be flown out Morag realised that she would have to make some sort of social life for herself. And Lauren, who had always been exactly the sort of popular, gay girl Morag had desired to be, would be the ideal person to see that she got one. Although she had been known as the naughtiest girl in the school, beneath the mischief there had been a warm heart, one that Morag remembered with gratitude. Lauren had tried to smooth Morag's path as much as she could.

'Good,' Lauren said happily. 'Perhaps Thorpe will bring you down some time. He and my Alan are always having earnest discussions over things like boundary fences and the more interesting diseases that affect sheep. They go hunting in the Mararuas together, too.'

Morag tried to summon up a picture of Thorpe, immaculate even in his work denims, sloping about the hills after wild pig, armed to the teeth like a brigand. She failed miserably.

'That would be lovely,' she replied rather lamely,

then, glancing at her watch, 'I'd better go as he said
he'd be back round about now. I'll see you soon,
Lauren.'

''Bye! And make sure you come down soon.'

There was no sign of Thorpe by the car, but a girl
in her late teens, Morag estimated, stood by the driver's
door, high heel tapping impatiently, her lovely face set
in an expression of haughty irritation as a group of
high school boys gave tongue to a very vocal appreciation of the car. Morag hesitated. Normally she would
have gone up and made herself known, but she had a
very strong feeling that the waiting girl would take
this as presumption. So she stared intently into the
window of the nearest shop while keeping a furtive
look-out for Thorpe's unmistakable figure coming up
the street.

Sure enough within five minutes he appeared in conversation with an elderly man who said his goodbye at
the car, nodded at the girl, then continued on up the
street. Morag realised that to avoid embarrassment she
should have lurked within the shop, but it was too late
to make such a move since he had seen her, so feeling
foolish she moved across the footpath.

There was no doubt that the girl who had waited
for him considered her very much in the way. Exquisitely beautiful with the proud imperiousness of a
Gainsborough painting, she fixed her large blue eyes on
to Morag's face and asked curtly, 'Who is this, Thorpe?'

For all the world, Morag thought, as if she was a
peasant who had just crawled out of the pig pen.

Not in the least thrown by her rudeness, Thorpe performed the introductions with suave charm.

She was Gabrielle Shaw and she was in love with
Thorpe, for after a perfunctory greeting to Morag she

turned her shoulder and began to ask him to dinner, her eyes fixed on his face in a gaze of hungry intensity which made Morag feel rather ashamed of her own sex, but profoundly sorry for the girl.

It must, she thought, be absolutely shattering to wear one's heart on one's sleeve in such a fashion. Especially as Thorpe showed no signs of reciprocating. Indeed, without Morag being entirely sure how he did it, he drew her back into orbit, as it were, so that Gabrielle Shaw had to invite her too. Which she did, in an ungracious, startled fashion, those immense blue eyes surveying her in one haughty, comprehensive glance, before fastening on Thorpe's face once again.

Morag had never been made to feel quite so small before. A sparkle irradiated the cool depths of her eyes as she refused the invitation politely but definitely.

'Never mind,' Gabrielle Shaw returned vaguely, immediately dismissing Morag to some limbo beyond thought. 'Thorpe, *do* say you can come! It's for my birthday.'

He ignored her, looking down at Morag with the smallest spark of anger in his glance. 'Why can't you come?' he asked smoothly, his hand on her shoulder in a gesture which was as possessive as it was intimate.

Without even looking Morag sensed the way the girl stiffened. Deciding that it was time to end this charade she said in a voice carefully neutral, 'I'm employed to look after Mrs Johnston's children, so I can hardly go out and leave her to cope.' Then she spoiled the effect by adding with a snap, 'Especially now, Thorpe!'

He dismissed this with a careless shrug. 'Gabrielle's birthday isn't for several weeks and Sally will have Hazel to help her. And for heaven's sake don't go giving her the idea that she's ill. She's not. Sarah said only that she *may* have valve trouble; it's certainly not definite.'

'What is this?' Gabrielle Shaw broke in impatiently. 'I'm sorry, but you seem to have left me behind. What's going on up at Wharuaroa, Thorpe?' Her glance beguiled him, hardened as it came to rest on Morag's troubled expression. 'Who has valve trouble?' And who, her tone implied, is this nursemaid you have in tow?

'Sally, my sister.' Thorpe's deep voice was casual as he told of the circumstances of Sally's wrist, finishing by saying, 'And this is Morag Nelson, who used to live at Wharuaroa years ago before she went Karitane nursing. She and Graham had a touching youthful romance, but are now both devoutly thankful that they didn't run away and get married!'

Morag found it easy enough to smile at him in answer to the pressure of his fingers on her shoulder. If he noticed the set quality of the smile he gave no sign.

'I see.' Gabrielle Shaw sounded uncertain, as well she might. Thorpe had managed to imply, more by manner than by words, that Morag was a friend of the family, and it was clear that Gabrielle had rethought her decision to ignore her.

'Surely Hazel can help your sister if she can't come too.' she said now. 'So that Miss—oh, Morag I'll call you as we're so informal up here—so that you can come too?'

There was no welcome in that china-blue regard, however, and Morag would once more have refused except that Thorpe took the words from her mouth.

'Of course she'll come too,' he said smoothly. 'She suffers from an overdose of conscientiousness, but I can cope with that.'

'I'm sure you can,' Gabrielle Shaw retorted, a smile of sweet malice on her beautifully painted lips. 'You can cope with most things, Thorpe. I'm sure Morag knows that.'

CHAPTER FOUR

As soon as he had started the engine he directed a taunting, sardonic glance at Morag's angry profile and said, 'Out with it, or you'll burst.'

Turning, she began heatedly, 'Well, you've got a nerve! I agreed to this—this *stupid* masquerade against my better judgment, but believe me, I had no idea you intended to spread the thing around the district! What on *earth* are you up to?'

'I should imagine it was obvious,' he said, curt by now as he in turn became angry. 'I dislike being pressured.'

'By the lovely Miss Shaw?' Morag lifted her brows at him, continuing sarcastically, 'I doubt very much whether you could get any other man to say that!'

'O.K., so I'm peculiar.' He smiled, rather unpleasantly. 'In several ways. Gabrielle is eighteen and of an obsessive nature. She came back home after three years away at school and decided that for her first big affair I should be the lucky man. As you know, adolescents give me a pain, especially those who imagine themselves in love. Unfortunately she's been completely spoiled by her doting parents.' He paused, and added drily, 'She can be quite enchanting when things are going her way, and as she's an only child I suppose one can't blame them.'

'God, you're patronising!'

'Oh, stop playing the injured party!' He sent her a narrowed, fierce glance, his mouth predatory. 'All right, so I'm using you, just as you used Graham and then me to get yourself out of a distasteful situation. I think you owe me this—reparation, if you like.'

'I paid you back!' she cried indignantly.

'The money, yes. You also irreparably ruined the relationship between my brother and me.'

On the verge of flatly denying this Morag paused. A note of bleak regret in the deep voice tugged at her sympathy. Rather gruffly she said, 'You weren't on good terms before I came on the scene, Thorpe.'

'After you left we weren't on any sort of terms at all,' he told her with brutal frankness. 'He blamed me for your departure, of course. Which reminds me of something I've often wondered. Why didn't you tell him about my interference in the letter you left for him?'

Thrown on to the defensive, she answered hastily, 'It wasn't for me—I didn't want to upset things too much.' After a moment she resumed, 'I felt guilty about taking the money, I suppose.'

'So you felt that you were as bad as I?' He grinned at that, reached out a hand which took one of hers and held it, letting her feel the strength of his fingers. Almost casually he said, 'We're two of a kind, you and me.'

'Now that,' she retorted, shaken by the strange wave of feeling which swept over her at his touch, '*that* I resent.'

He laughed, a compellingly attractive sound in the intimacy of the car. 'Resent or not, it happens to be the truth.'

Fortunately for Morag's peace of mind the road wound up the side of a gully, involving some rather skilful driving. Thorpe replaced her hand on her lap so that he could concentrate on the corners, his features once more aloof and withdrawn, a handsome mask to cover his thoughts.

When she went down to dinner that night Morag found herself thinking that six years could create a vast change in circumstances. In the past she would not have known how to behave on an occasion such as this; she would have been nervously gauche and quite unable to summon up any poise. So the dinner, even an informal one like this, would have been an ordeal. But then six years ago she would not have been invited into the house.

That still rankled, after all these years. It was, she thought, one of the reasons why she resented Thorpe Cunningham as much as she was attracted to him, because of that callous disregard for her younger self. And telling herself that of course his first loyalty was to his brother and his family did nothing to ease that resentment!

In spite of her confident bearing there was an odd little coldness in the pit of her stomach which intensified just outside the door to the drawing room. Mindful of Thorpe's orders she had put on a pale honey silk jersey blouse, a beautiful thing which had made an inordinate hole in her bank balance a few months before. It clung, revealing the graceful lines of her body above a skirt in a pattern of barbaric golds and blues and corals. The effect was casual yet sophisticated, and she hoped that that was just how she looked, too. It should have given her confidence, but these people took exquisite clothes for granted.

Thorpe was in the room alone, standing beside a bookcase with a book in his hand, reading. He looked up as she came in, appreciation and something else giving warmth to the blue-green of his glance. Acutely self-conscious, Morag found herself walking stiff-legged, like a cat at the arrival of something that threatens it.

'Very nice,' he said drily, putting the book down.

'Almost from the sublime to the ridiculous. Or *vice versa.*'

Allowing herself a slight lifting of the shoulders, Morag said, 'You did make your wishes quite clear.'

'Oh, I'm glad you had something you could wear.' It was a taunt, as was the comprehensive sweep of his glance over her face and body, lingering rather too long to be polite on her mouth and the soft roundness of her breasts.

The heat in her cheeks seemed to amuse him, but when she stayed obstinately silent, he forbore to taunt her any longer and poured her a drink, and then with that abrupt change of manner which bewildered her showed her a colour plate in the book he had been looking at.

It was the Annunciation, mediaeval and quaint yet saturated with the piety of those days. The Angel carried a long stalk of Madonna lilies, the Maiden herself was grave and decorous, a golden halo around her head, her robe that superb blue which bears her name. In the background was an idealised landscape, charming in blues and soft greens. Around the centre painting was an elaborate border of leaves and flowers and scrolls, enclosing much smaller paintings of angels playing various musical instruments. It was enchanting.

Morag said so, her pleasure evident in the absorbed interest of her expression as she bent over the page.

'It's a page from one of the mediaeval Books of Hours,' Thorpe told her. 'Have you seen one before?'

'No.' She smiled suddenly, her whole face alight with humour. 'I'm afraid my artistic education has been sadly neglected. In the immortal words, I don't know anything about art, but I know what I like!'

He grinned, and turned the page, revealing more

enchantments. 'Feel free to borrow anything you want to. As for your artistic education, these are a fairly sophisticated form of art, once you've become used to the conventions that held sway over the art world in those days. So your eye, though untutored, is a good one.'

Such praise, if praise it could be called, filled Morag with an elation as treacherous as it was unexpected. It was a relief when Graham and Louise came in then, and she could turn away from Thorpe and greet them, meet the suspicion and mistrust in Louise's pale blue gaze with an equanimity she was far from feeling.

At first it seemed that the evening was going to be a nightmare, but Thorpe saved the situation. Somehow, by some mysterious magic of personality, he managed to overcome the cross-currents which would have caused a less poised man to founder; it was not hard to follow his lead and in a very short time Morag felt a lot of the tenseness seep out of her as she made laboured but polite conversation with Louise whose innate good manners forced her to follow suit.

It was hard work, however. A second surprise in the appearance of Lauren Ramsgate and her Alan, a tall, fair giant of a man with one blue eye and one brown, relaxed Morag even more. Their arrival resulted in more conversation, general this time, and then it was time for dinner.

Never at a loss for a conversational topic, Lauren followed Thorpe's lead with relish; possibly it was the wine, which he seemed rather free with, or more likely Lauren's infectious good humour, but by the time they had finished the delicious mixture of fresh fruit and liqueur which Hazel had dreamed up as dessert, they were all relaxed and cheerful, even Louise and Graham.

Morag was glad. Furious though she was with Graham for telling lies about their relationship in the past, her anger had not lasted past the one pleading, abject glance he had sent her at the beginning of the evening. It was easy to see that he lived in some private hell where no one could reach him except the woman who had put him there. And she was not happy, either, her hands restless and always moving, touching her rings, her necklace, fingers against her temple as though in pain, twisting together in her lap.

Looking up, Morag met Thorpe's eyes, direct and unreadable, and felt a tingle of awareness through her veins. Seated at the head of his table, he was completely master of the situation, long fingers curled around the stem of his wine glass as he leaned back to survey these people who danced to his bidding.

For they were all in his power, except for the Ramsgates. Yet even they had obeyed his summons. He needed them for their uncomplicated good humour, and as witnesses that Morag Nelson was his latest interest. For a moment she hated him, and then he smiled at her and the hatred was swamped by an emotion she could not define, never having felt it before.

Oh, my heavens! she thought in desperation. I think I'm falling in love with the man!

His hand covered hers and he stood up, more or less pulling her with him. Morag caught Lauren's openly interested glance and blushed, but allowed herself to be led out, contenting herself with one speaking, glittering look which only he could see.

As if in retaliation, he kept her beside him for the rest of the evening. He was not obvious in his attentions; Thorpe Cunningham was not an obvious man; but there could be no doubt that he was playing his part extremely well. No doubt, Morag thought nastily, he had behaved like this a hundred times before, attentive to all of his guests yet making one woman feel that she was the focus of his interest. How he did it she wasn't prepared to say, for after that loose handclasp he did not touch her again, but there could be no denying that he got his message across.

Whether she was as good an actor she didn't know. With any luck enough of that reluctant attraction was revealed so that she appeared to be falling for him.

Altogether a wearying evening, and she was heartily glad to see the guests go. When the door closed behind Louise and Graham it was with relief that she turned to climb the stairs, but Thorpe said, 'Wait a moment, I've something to say to you. Come back into the drawing room where we won't be overheard.'

Nerves stretched tautly, she preceded him into the room, stopping just inside the door.

'Well?' she asked defensively.

'Oh, very well.' He looked down at her, defiance in every line of her small, slender body, and drawled, 'That should give them all something to think about. The next step, I imagine, is that Lauren will warn you.'

Her brows shot heavenwards. '*Warn* me?'

'Yes. I noticed a rather worried gleam in her eye on occasions. No doubt, as a member of the sisterhood, she'll feel obliged to tell you that a man of thirty-one who isn't married is a poor security risk.' He spoke with a mocking, derisive note in his voice as if he wished to anger her—or perhaps, himself.

Morag looked at his shirt button. 'O.K. I'll give my celebrated imitation of a woman rushing in where angels fear to tread.' Then her flippancy left her and she met his gaze, lifting her head so that the subdued light fell on her face. 'Thorpe, do you think it fooled your sister-in-law?'

'She's constitutionally suspicious, but yes, I think she is starting to believe our fiction.' He spoke moodily, his mouth compressed so that he looked cruel and more than a little ruthless.

Instinctively Morag stepped back. In a lightning-swift movement he caught her shoulder and held her there, his fingers moving slowly over the heavy silk of her blouse.

'Thorpe . . .' she began, half under her breath.

'Morag.' It was said in mockery, but there was no mockery in the way he brought her close to him, and when he kissed her the mockery had gone entirely, leaving in its place a desire which beat against the walls of her resistance, threatening to overwhelm her.

Afterwards she would ask herself why this one man, and only he, had the power to shock her into passion, but when his mouth touched hers all sanity fled, and she could only respond, winding her hands in his hair, giving of herself with an ardour she had never dreamed she possessed.

When he lifted her and carried her across to the sofa as if she were a child she did not fight, nor did she flinch when his hand moved from the skin at her waist, sliding up beneath the silk to find her breasts. Then she lifted her eyes to his, her own glazed yet wondering, and he smiled and kissed her again, exerting such a mastery over her senses that she was lost.

It took the click of the door to bring her back to herself. Thorpe looked across the room, his expression set in lines of hauteur that chilled her, exposed as she was to Louise's eyes.

'Try knocking next time,' he said curtly, turning Morag slightly so that she was half hidden by his shoulder. 'I'm sorry.' Louise sounded oddly breathless. 'I left my bag behind.'

There was a quick scurry of footsteps and then she was gone, calling out an embarrassed 'Goodnight' as she left.

Thorpe looked down at Morag's scarlet face and released her as she struggled to move away, more humiliated by this incident than she had ever been by anything.

'Don't look so self-conscious,' he said tauntingly. 'Consider it all a part of the plot. If she wasn't convinced before she certainly is now.'

A dreadful suspicion assailed her, bringing with it shame and hot anger. Moving very carefully, she slid her feet into her shoes and began to tuck in her blouse while self-contempt washed over her in coldly sickening waves. She could see only one way of salving the tattered remnants of her pride and took it, keeping her voice as casual in tone as she could.

'What made you think she would come back?' she asked, summoning up the last remnants of her strength to look across at him.

For a second he looked a trifle surprised, then smiled, a slow unpleasant movement of his lips which revealed just how correct her suspicions had been.

'Let's just say that I know women,' he murmured. 'Also I noticed that she'd gone out without her bag. Louise is inordinately careful of her belongings.'

Morag nodded, surprised at the steadiness of her movements. 'How very experienced you are! I wondered, of course, but that's because I'm a woman.'

'Meaning that that's how you would have behaved? Come sneaking back to spy on lovers?' He looked at her as though she was something small and unpleasant he had found under a microscope.

Morag managed a jaunty grin, stood up and began to smooth the velvet of her skirt over her hips. 'If I wanted to know badly enough, probably.'

'God, you women!' Rising, he did not attempt to hide the open contempt in his voice. 'Is this how you behaved with Graham, pandering to his lust yet using that cool brain of yours to calculate exactly how much you could gain from it!'

'Just like you,' she said lightly. 'You were quite right when you said we were two of a kind.' Although her heart felt as if it were breaking under the load of disillusionment some perverse demon drove her on to add, 'Don't tell me that I shock you, Thorpe. I thought you a little more experienced than that! Surely it doesn't come as too much of a surprise to know that women are quite capable of experiencing passion without love. And why do you constantly hark back to my relationship with Graham? It's almost as though you have a *thing* about it.'

Immediately she knew that she had gone too far. He had been listening to her with his expression set in the lines of proud hauteur which had so intimidated Louise, but at this last comment, tossed in because she felt she must attack him somehow to wipe the taste of defeat from her, his face changed, because grim and purposeful and frighteningly hard.

'Perhaps,' he said so softly that she had to strain to hear him, 'Perhaps I have. Perhaps I wanted you then as I want you now. Come here.'

Staring, she saw where her stupid bravado had led her, straight into a situation where she could only be the loser. Some instinct warned her not to resist him physically, for there was such a predatory smile on his mouth as he approached her that she knew he would enjoy using his superior strength to subdue her to his will.

With a poise she had never known she possessed

she shrugged, saying calmly, 'I find you attractive, too. However, I don't intend to allow it to upset my life. If I leaped into bed with every man I found interesting I'd have no time to do anything else.'

Hoping fervently that this nonsense was close enough to the truth to fool him, she looked directly up, allowing what she prayed was a glint of mockery to appear in her glance.

'You're a cool customer,' he said, sardonically appreciative. One hand reached out to fasten itself around a knot of hair at the nape of her neck, holding her quiescent. 'With a ready tongue, quick enough to get you out of most trouble, I imagine. Are you as hard as you seem to be, Morag?'

'Every bit,' she supplied cheerfully, but oh, her heart was sore with the punishment he had given it and she hated him, *hated* him for the masculine arrogance which allowed him to kiss her as if he meant it just to fool Louise, yet despised her because he thought she was doing the same. He was dangerous, far too dangerous for her peace of mind, but she could not possibly fall in love with a man who was such a chauvinist. Small consolation, when her heart beat wildly in her breast and she wanted above all other things to feel the pressure of that cruel mouth on hers, the sensuous pleasure that his touch sent through her nerves!

He smiled crookedly down at her and bent his head to touch her lips with his, a swift, light pressure which teased rather than satisfied, then released her, saying calmly, 'Well, we'll see. In the meantime, you'd better get some sleep.'

Although she went to her bedroom she did not, of course, sleep. After what seemed hours of tossing and turning she got up to look out of the window, and saw beneath her on the freshly mown grass a square of light which showed that Thorpe was still in his study. A quick glance at her watch showed that it was well after one in the morning.

Feeling rather pleased that he too was awake, Morag went back to bed where of course she fell soundly into a deep slumber.

The weather decided to turn nasty the next morning so that by lunchtime the skies were a leaden grey with every sign pointing to a downpour. Sally was up and about, her usual cheerful self, but did not join Morag and the boys in the long brisk walk they took down to a stream and back, saying that she preferred to stay inside out of the cold.

Warmly wrapped in plaid jackets, wearing long trousers and absurd woolly hats on their heads, the boys chattered to each other as they strode through the grass, exhibiting a quite extensive knowledge of farm life which surprised Morag. It was obvious from their conversation that they spent quite a lot of their time at Wharuaroa. Not for the first time Morag wondered at her employer's marriage. Sally was quite obviously devoted to her husband, but what sort of man would leave his wife with three small children and head off to Antarctica to spend the winter?

It was not, she thought wryly, the sort of marriage she would like. A husband was for sharing things with. In which case it was to be hoped that she didn't fall in love with a man who had made the Navy his career!

Hands deep in the pockets of her coat, for the wind came from the west and was keen, she looked around her with pleasure. The dark clouds and thunderous atmosphere gave the grass an eerie greenness which fascinated her; the boys' voices rang out clearly, almost shrilly. Everything was very lush and fertile-looking, but behind stood the high hills, many covered by primeval bush, others of which had been fired and then left to go back into scrub. They were white with the flowers of manuka bushes, the early settlers' tea-tree, for they used its tiny aromatic leaves as a substitute for their favourite drink. The gold was gorse blossom, the curse of these northern hills, introduced by those same early settlers for fodder and hedging. It had run wild and only recently, Morag knew, had the battle against it and other invaders such as bramble and sweetbriar and hawthorn been won with the help of herbicides of extreme potency.

Not that there was any sign of any such villains on Thorpe's land. The gently rounded hills and valleys were dotted with totara and puriri trees to give shelter; they lent a parklike air to the landscape. And each stream on his property had its banks well held by a ribbon of native growth preventing the erosion which scarred so much of New Zealand's landscape.

Morag turned, admiring. No one could deny that the Cunninghams had farmed with a sensitivity for the land which too few farmers possessed. She couldn't blame Graham for not wanting to leave such pastoral beauty, just as she did not blame Thorpe for refusing to divide the station in two, but it did occur to her that their father had left things arranged a little unfairly.

Or perhaps not, she thought, remembering Graham's febrile nervousness of manner last night, his air of being strung on wires, the dislike for his brother which was never far below the surface. He had revealed it often, in remarks which were meant to be humorous and weren't, in cracks which had been aimed directly at Thorpe. Morag rather thought that had she been their father she, too, would have made sure that Thorpe got the station. Graham was too easily swayed by his emotions to make a safe guardian for Wharu-aroa's lovely acres.

The creek was tiny, a stony-bottomed stream which announced its position some yards away by a great chattering of water. Morag breathed deeply, enjoying the damp, leafy scent, the icy coldness of the water on her hand when she felt it to please her charges. For such inveterate dabblers they were quite happy to keep out of it once they had felt it and shocked Morag with a few drops carefully sprinkled on her face.

Laughing, she pretended to chase them, then walked through the trees with one on each side, admiring their finds, a pretty greeny stone, a dandelion flower and once a leopard slug, a massive thing about two inches long which they found under some rotting bark. Re-pressing a shudder, Morag admired it, then suggested that perhaps it wasn't fair to take the slug away from its home. With the best will in the world Sally was in-clined to shriek at Daddy-long-legs! How she would react to a leopard slug, Morag didn't know and wasn't prepared to put to the test.

'O.K.,' Richie said cheerfully, echoed by his brother. Very tenderly they deposited the gruesome thing in the exact spot where they had found it and set off homewards.

'We'd better hurry, chaps,' said Morag, after one ex-perienced glance at the sky. 'It's going to rain any minute. I'll race you up to the house!'

'O.K.! Bet we beat,' they said, and set off, short legs pumping them along through the grass.

Halfway up the hill the sound of the tractor coming up fast behind them made Morag grab a hand of each and slow into a walk.

It was Graham, with a trailer on behind. 'Hop up,' he yelled, jerking his head behind.

Morag shook her head vigorously, 'No, thanks,' and repeated it more loudly when he looked incredulous. Shrugging, he roared off towards the sheds.

'Why not, Morag? Why not?' Jason demanded, tugging at her hand.

'Tractors are dangerous, my love. Very dangerous for little people.'

Satisfied with her answer, they set off once more, skirting the cattle pens and the sheds, setting the dogs barking as they tore by, then through the gate into the garden and up the steps to the back door.

'Just made it,' said Hazel from the door of the freezer room. 'If you get those boots off and ask Morag nicely, I'll let you into my kitchen.' She winked at Morag.

'Ooh!' Small strong hands pulled at gumboots, deposited them neatly in the row with all the others, after which there was a rush to the basin to wash their hands.

Morag grinned at the housekeeper, having arrived at an understanding with her about snacks, then her heart lurched as Thorpe came out of the now heavy rain stripping off his wet shirt as he walked through the door. Like that, his skin sleeked by raindrops, his hair darkened to almost red-black, he looked piratical and altogether too male for any woman's peace of mind.

The boys called out to him, asking him to plead with Morag to allow them into the kitchen, and he grinned, his eyes alight as though he had enjoyed the short tussle with the elements.

'I was *never* allowed in the kitchen,' he informed them provocatively, without a hint of teasing except the glint in his glance.

There was a short silence while the boys digested this, then Richie, always the bolder, ventured diffidently, 'Hazel *likes* us in her kitchen. Truly, Uncle Thorpe.'

'Then who am I to stop you? Just don't eat her scones.'

'We won't!'

Hands dried helter-skelter, they followed the house-keeper down the passage towards the kitchen leaving Morag alone with him, oddly ill at ease, so that she was not quite sure of how to get out of the room without giving him cause for one of the taunts he excelled at making.

He seemed to enjoy her wariness, for he sent her a jeering smile, one which made the hair on the back of her neck lift.

Abruptly she said, 'I'd better go with them.'

'Hazel is quite able to see that they don't spoil their lunch.' He emerged from the room they called the washroom, towelling his hair. 'Don't go. I want to talk to you.'

Morag contented herself with lifting her delicate brows, but she made no further attempt to leave, well aware that the excitement which beat in her breast like a suffocating bird must reveal itself in some way in her expression. It was humiliating that after last night's fiasco she should respond to him so easily, but she was a realist, and knew that this desire of the eye was no respecter of persons. After all, in spite of the fact that he despised her, Thorpe was just as conscious of the tug of attraction between them as she was.

As if to reinforce this dreary conclusion he said abruptly, 'I'm sorry if I was harsh with you last night. I dislike deception.'

Morag felt her brows climb towards her hairline.

'You could have fooled me,' she commented drily. 'I thought you were enjoying it.'

'Does it rankle?' He smiled savagely and tossed the towel on to a chair, running his fingers through his hair to reduce it to some sort of order.

Hardening her heart against his effect on her, she shrugged, saying coolly, 'No, but the way you take advantage of a perfectly normal reaction does rankle.'

'Oh?' He caught her up quickly, a glint of sardonic humour in his glance. 'What perfectly normal reaction?'

'Oh, come on now, Thorpe! Don't pretend to be obtuse. You know exactly what I mean.'

'You know, you bewilder me,' he said softly, his eyes very sharp as they scrutinised her face.

'On the surface you look a prim little thing, perhaps a bit repressed, and yet you respond to me like a wanton and in the next breath behave like a cool, sophisticated, rather tough woman of the world. Which is the real Morag Nelson?'

Allowing irony to colour her voice, she returned crisply, 'I find it hard to believe that you feel any interest in my personality.' With subtle emphasis on the last word she made it obvious where she thought his interests lay, she had the satisfaction of seeing his mouth tighten as her shaft hit home.

Turning, she finished over her shoulder, 'And there's no need to apologise. Believe me, I'm about as interested in you as you are in me, and for roughly the same reason. You've got a hold over me, one you have no intention of relinquishing at the present, and I'll go along with that. But don't expect me to fall in love with you, or be so stupid as to expect anything from you at all. I'm not interested in an affair, either.'

'There you go again,' he said softly from behind her. 'A really tough chick.'

She stiffened as his arm caught her around the waist.

'There's no one to see now,' she said hardily.

'So? I couldn't care less.'

'I will not be made a—a convenience of!' Eyes sparkling with temper and—yes, excitement, she jerked herself away, was inexorably hauled back against him and felt his lips touch her skin below her ear before he laughed softly and let her go.

'Well, seeing that you've been so frank I'll reciprocate in kind,' he said casually to her rigid back. 'I find you very attractive, but I'm a fastidious man.'

'Meaning?'

'Just that I don't like second-hand goods.'

The calculated cruelty of it drove the blood from her face. One fist clenched against her side and in a stifled voice, she retorted, 'If that's an example of your fastidiousness, heaven preserve me from your rudeness!'

He ground out an expletive, fortunately muffled, and swung her around to face him, his hands ungentle on her shoulders.

'Tears?' He touched one glittering drop, and said harshly, 'God knows why, but you bring out the worst in me. I'm sorry—and this time don't throw my apology back in my face!'

Always he had the power to bewilder her. With a crooked attempt at a smile she responded, 'I don't think I dare. You say you don't understand me; I'll return the compliment. I don't understand you, Thorpe, not one little bit.'

'And yet you should,' he said half below his breath, his regard very piercing as it swept her features, lingering on them with none of the boldness she found so distasteful. 'Unless you really are an innocent.'

'And of course I couldn't be that, as you've pointed out so frequently,' she said, weary of the conversation and the tight rein his closeness was forcing her to hold on her reactions. Looking up, she met the intensity of his blue-green gaze, saw the twist of contemptuous mockery that her words brought to his lips, and broke away, wondering why she should hate the fact that he thought her once Graham's mistress.

'Don't answer that,' she said carelessly, in as cool a voice as she could manage. 'When is Sally going for her tests?'

'The day after tomorrow.'

'So soon?'

'Yes.' He turned away, saying curtly, 'Rachel goes with us, but I'll leave you in charge of the twins.'

She nodded, her own turmoil forgotten in the greater worry of Sally's health. 'Thorpe, just what will it involve?'

'Tests. X-rays mainly. If they have to do an operation she'll have to wean Rachel, of course, and you'll be in charge of her as well as the boys.'

'Will they do it straight away?'

'I imagine so.' He turned back to face her and she saw worry and indecision in his expression, completely at variance with the strength of his features. 'She's quite adamant that we don't contact Sandy.'

In a way it was a request for help. Without stopping to wonder why this uncharacteristic weakness should so affect her, Morag said swiftly, 'She's right, Thorpe. There's absolutely nothing he can do, and surely, if you do get in touch with him she'll be upset. And that will be bad for her.'

'Oh, I've told myself that.' He hesitated, his expression bleak, then went on, 'If I were Sally and she—well, she didn't make it through the op., I would never forgive those who kept the knowledge of her illness from me.'

'Yes, but Sally's husband sounds a vastly different

character from you.' Morag met the chill comprehension of his eyes without flinching, continuing, 'You can't judge him by what you would do, Thorpe. And give Sally the credit for knowing what's right for her —and for him.'

He continued to look down at her, almost as if she wasn't there, then shrugged slightly. Morag thought that for a moment he had forgotten who she was and had been tempted to confide in her, but she might have been mistaken. It wasn't like the Thorpe Cunningham she knew to show such weakness.

Aloofly he retorted, 'Well, as you said, if I go against her wishes I'll upset her, and at the moment we can't afford to do that.'

CHAPTER FIVE

FORTUNATELY for Morag's peace of mind Thorpe took
Sally through to Auckland the next day, driving her
down by car as it was not thought advisable for her to
fly.

As she walked back into the house after waving them
goodbye Morag mused on Sally's cheerfulness. First
appearances were deceptive, for her employer had
seemed a lightweight, one of life's butterflies. Yet she
had taken the news of her possible condition with a
calmness which did her credit. Concealed beneath that
rather frivolous exterior Sally obviously had a considerable amount of the Cunningham backbone. Morag
found herself hoping fervently that the tests would reveal nothing, and was astonished at the depths of her
emotion. Really, she thought wryly, taking Richie's
cold little hand in hers, these Cunninghams had something, a kind of fatal fascination for her. First Graham,
then Sally, and now this potent attraction that drew
her to Thorpe. Had she possessed any sense of self-
preservation at all she would have flatly refused to come
back to Wharuaroa!

The boys were fretful without their mother's presence, and as the day decided to prove just how miserable life could be by pouring with rain, a real
Northland downpour, it took a fair amount of Morag's
ingenuity to prevent squabbles. In the end she and
Hazel joined forces and in the pleasure of making
dough in the big, warm kitchen, childish worries were
forgotten.

Hazel poured tea and they sat at one end of the table and gossiped as the boys rolled industrially at the other.

'Do you think she'll be all right?'

Morag smiled. 'Hazel, I'm a Karitane nurse, nothing more. I'd say that if spirit gets you anywhere, and it does, she'll be fit as a trout this time next year, even if they do have to replace any valves.'

'Oh, they've all got spirit. At least, except for Graham. Honestly, I could *kick* him sometimes!'

Morag chuckled, for the housekeeper's normally cheerful expression was replaced by diabolical anger, or as close a simulation of it as she could manage.

'I mean it,' Hazel stated glumly. 'Has he changed much since you knew him?'

Startled, Morag looked up. It was apparent that Hazel knew all about that long-ago romance; she would, of course. In a place like Wharuaroa gossip travelled quickly. 'I don't know that I ever really knew him,' she answered after a moment, choosing her words carefully. 'We were both very young.'

'I just wondered if he'd always been the same. Ah well, he'll be up here before long, he and that wife of his, behaving as if they owned the place.' Then apparently feeling she had said enough, Hazel changed the subject firmly, leaving Morag a prey to doubts and conjectures.

The boys were difficult to settle after lunch, but when Jason had at last dropped off to sleep Morag found herself with nothing to do, an occasion almost unprecedented!

After writing two letters to friends, she remembered Thorpe's invitation to make use of any books she wanted and set off down the staircase. Outside it was still raining, a relentless, heavy downpour which was typical of Northland's sub-tropical climate, where it could tip out three inches of rain in half an hour. That was in exceptional circumstances, but even so, to-morrow there would be floods in the valleys and the clear waters of the Bay of Islands would be discoloured with the red-brown volcanic silt brought down by the flooded rivers.

Acutely conservation-minded, Hazel always turned off lights as she went through the house, so Morag had to grope her way down the hall and into the big sitting room. Panelling was beautiful, she thought, but it certainly made for gloom on days like this.

She was halfway across to the bookcase when she realised that she was not alone in the room. Louise stood with her back to the door, an exquisite flame Doulton vase in her hands, and the expression on her face one of hopeless longing.

For a moment Morag stood, irresolute, and then turned and snapped a table lamp on, so that when Louise whirled around she found Morag apparently in the act of turning too.

Hoping fervently that Louise's astonishment was mirrored in her own features, Morag grinned, saying loudly above the persistent din of the rain outside, 'I'm sorry, I didn't see you. Did I startle you?'

'You did.' Putting the vase back on to the mantel, Louise asked abruptly, 'What are you doing here?'

Morag's hackles lifted, but she forced herself to answer pleasantly, 'I've come to borrow a book.'

'Oh.' The other woman looked at the bookcase before her narrowed glance swung back to Morag. 'Did Thorpe give you permission?'

'Of course.'

'Then go ahead, get one. Though I'd have thought

that your days at least should be given to your work.'

There was nothing to be said to this piece of calculated rudeness, for Morag refused to rush to defend herself. Forcing herself to move naturally, she chose a book, a modern novel she had wanted to read for some months, and said lightly, 'This will do very nicely.'

Louise's unblinking gaze made her profoundly uneasy, it was so unnatural. Morag found it hard to turn her back on the other woman, but she certainly wasn't going to stay trading stares with her, so she said, 'I'll see you later, perhaps.'

Still no answer. With the tiniest of shrugs Morag made her way to the door, feeling between her shoulder-blades the intensity of the other woman's stare.

Just as she got to the door Louise called harshly, 'Wait, I—come back here.'

Morag turned, one eyebrow lifting at the peremptory yet almost pleading tone of the woman's voice. Without moving from the doorway she asked remotely, 'Yes?'

Graham's wife had a guarded, intense expression, as though she was driven by some imperative need to the step she was taking. Pale eyes blazing with the depth of her emotions, she managed to keep full control over her voice. 'Just what is the situation between you and Thorpe?' she demanded curtly.

Hesitating, Morag wondered what would most convince Louise, and decided after a fraction of a second of rapid thought that she would act as naturally as if she and Thorpe were truly attracted to each other.

'I'm afraid that's no business of yours,' she returned gently, but with a note of firmness in her voice which made Louise flush angrily.

'God, but you're cool!' Nervously she crossed her

arms, rubbing her hands against the opposing fore-arms. 'It must have been a shock to discover that Graham was married.'

A lie was definitely needed here. 'I already knew,' Morag told her distantly. 'I've been with Mrs Johnston for some weeks.'

Louise nodded, her expression set in lines of rigid control. 'Yes, I suppose so. If you knew, why did you come back?'

'Certainly not to break up your marriage,' Morag told her bluntly, feeling exasperation and profound compassion in roughly equal measures. 'Believe me, Mrs Cunningham, if I'd wanted your husband I'd have married him six years ago, when he thought he was in love with me.'

The blonde head jerked back as if a phantom hand had struck the lovely cheek. Louise stared at Morag, breathing deeply, her eyes unfocussed. After a moment she seemed to regain command of herself. With a swift movement she sank into a chair, her fingers at the gold locket she wore at her throat as if it was a lifeline.

'You shouldn't have come back,' she said slowly.

Some instinct, perhaps based on her nursing training, perhaps inborn, told Morag that Louise was no-where near as neurotic as she liked to be considered. There had been a gleam of calculation in those blue eyes as she spoke, as though she was watching the effect her behaviour was having on Morag.

Very crisply she returned, 'I don't see why not,' and remembering what she had said to Thorpe, continued, 'New Zealand is a very small place, Mrs Cunningham. So small that it was almost inevitable that I meet up with your husband again. If every woman here had to avoid her former boy-friends we'd all have to take to the bush and live like hermits!'

'But it was not just a youthful affair, was it?' Louise said harshly. 'You were lovers.'

With a gesture which was fierce in its repudiation Morag retorted, 'I'm sick to death of being cast as the scarlet adulteress in the Cunningham family drama! Just think of one thing, Mrs Cunningham. Does Thorpe strike you as the sort of man who would take his brother's leavings?'

It was a daring move, bringing Thorpe into the conversation, but Morag could think of no other way of convincing the wretched woman that she was wrong. Mentally deciding that the sooner she had things out with Graham the better, she went on with less heat, 'I have no interest in your husband, Mrs Cunningham, or he in me. And if you're going to hound me with accusations and scenes I'll have to tell Thorpe about it.'

Another even more daring move, but like the first, one which worked. Thorpe's name seemed to be a magic talisman!

Louise looked at her with honest hatred, becoming much more human as she said, 'Oh, you think you've got Thorpe on a string! Well, let me tell you that he'll never marry you! He's going to marry Gabrielle Shaw.'

One of Morag's mobile brows climbed, but she contented herself with saying calmly, 'Time will tell. Now, if you'll excuse me—the children may be stirring.'

It wasn't until she was halfway up the stairs that she realised that she was trembling with reaction.

But even though the ugly little scene appalled her she could not rid herself of the idea that beneath that neurotic veneer Graham's wife cultivated there was a very cool, astute brain. Perhaps it was one way of keeping her husband dancing attendance on her, perhaps she had allowed herself to drift into a pose through boredom and discontent; surely she could see that she was accomplishing nothing by her actions?

Unless, perhaps, she was working towards some goal, some plan she had made.

Up in her area of the house Morag checked the two sleeping boys before sitting down in the rocking chair with the novel she had chosen, but she found it impossible to concentrate, and after reading the first page several times she left it open in her lap and stared out of the window.

It was still raining. Lord, she thought, I'd forgotten that rain could be so heavy! In the South Island it tended to be more misty and much lighter. Here it was as if a giant was pouring buckets of water straight down on to the ground beneath. Uneasily she considered Louise, who had been the cause of the whole situation. Things were quite complicated enough, with Thorpe impinging far too much on her thoughts and feelings, without Louise making more trouble.

Then the boys woke and the afternoon went, and after dinner, when the rain had eased off a little, Thorpe rang from Auckland. The sound of his voice sent an odd little quiver through Morag's veins, but she matched his businesslike tones with her own, and when he relinquished the phone to Sally it was a relief to her.

'Everything's fine,' Sally assured her. 'We went to see the specialist, Mr Jameson, this afternoon. He's a darling, an old friend of Mum's. And he seemed cautiously optimistic, you know the way they are. He said that Sarah Griffiths was right to send me down but perhaps things weren't quite as bad as they looked. I'm all hopeful, but Thorpe is being his usual down-to-earth self. Anyway, I'll go into hospital feeling much more cheerful.'

Which was a good thing. Sally had hidden her fears,

but there was no doubt that she had been frightened. Naturally so, Morag thought. It would be terrifying to one as young and vital as Sally.

The next few days were a curious hiatus, a time when the weather eased up and spring became once more apparent in the softer warmth of the days and the flowering of the garden into its lushest growth. There were still freesias and daffodils about, but the camellias began to fade as nasturtiums and pelargoniums and sparaxias flaunted their vivid, brighter colours. Between the flagstones of the terrace the thyme flowered, its gay lilac spikes attracting early bees. Bearded iris lifted their regal orchid-like flowers, their rich vanilla scent wafting over the garden.

The boys made friends with the pet lambs, three of them hand-reared by Hazel but old enough to live in the house paddock. They considered themselves to be human and met the boys with loud eager bleats and an invitation to play. The twins adored them and when offered the big bottle of warm milk by Hazel enjoyed nothing more than hanging grimly on to them as the lambs sucked with eager enthusiasm, little tails wriggling with what seemed to be independent energy.

The house seemed empty without Thorpe. And without Sally and Rachel too, Morag reminded herself firmly.

And then they were home again, Sally thinner but still gay, Thorpe with that air of constraint lifted, looking at once younger and infinitely more approachable and unfortunately even more handsome.

'No nasty valve trouble,' Sally told them vivaciously. 'He said I was tired, and rather gave me to believe that it was partly that I'm missing Sandy very badly. But my heart is O.K.—sound as a bell. He's written to Dr Griffiths and I have to go and see her soon so that she can prescribe things. But I have to exercise a bit more and eat a bit more. He was a dear, wasn't he, Thorpe; he said that he liked his women a little plumper than modern fashion decreed, and I could do with an extra few pounds on, provided it's good muscle!'

'Well, that's a relief,' Hazel exclaimed, pouring another cup of tea. 'And how was the baby while you were in hospital?'

'Spoiled rotten!' Sally gave Rachel an adoring smile. They aren't used to healthy babes and they loved her. She was so good. No tears at all.'

Later, when the twins were enthusing over the toys their mother had brought back to them, Thorpe said quietly to Morag, 'Everything O.K.?'

It was the first time he had spoken directly to her and she had been a little piqued because he had almost ignored her, after a first piercing look which seemed to penetrate the innermost recesses of her brain.

With a note of reservation she replied, 'Yes, everything's fine.'

'Good.' He slanted a considering glance down towards her, his expression mocking yet not unkind. 'I'm not letting you off your promise to stay with Sally until her husband comes back.'

The tiniest of shrugs lifted her shoulders. 'I'm not stupid. I can see for myself that she isn't fit enough to cope with the children alone.'

'She's run down, and like a twit hasn't got herself back into shape after Rachel. She needs looking after more than the twins.'

He looked suddenly forbidding. Morag wondered if he was thinking of the absent Sandy, and said hurriedly, 'Well, spring's here, Thorpe. And I'll take her for nice long walks each day.'

'If it's fine,' he said, grinning as a sudden sharp shower sent Hazel tearing from the room, crying, 'My *washing*!'

Rather glad to be given the excuse, Morag followed her. As they unpegged the clothes from the rotary hoist she couldn't help thinking that in some subtle way she seemed to be becoming a part of life here at Wharuaroa, far more than she had ever been anywhere else. She fitted in, in spite of what Louise and Thorpe and Gabrielle Shaw might think, which was distinctly odd, when she considered the fact that she had hated the two years she had spent here in her adolescence.

It blew up an easterly gale overnight, a cool brisk wind, which had none of the icy chill of winds from the south and west. True to her word, Morag muffled Sally up well and took her, protesting rather feebly, down the road which led from the implement sheds towards the hills at the back of the farm.

It was only partly cloudy, great galleons of white and grey racing across a sky which had lost the icy clearness of winter and had a touch of the warm blue which was a sign of summer not too far away. The air was crisp, a pleasure to breathe, especially when it was perfumed by the fringe-like hakea blossoms on one of the shelter belts. On the hills the strident gold of the gorse merged with the softer buff of the kumarohe bushes, now in full flower.

'The Maoris and bushmen used to use the kumarahoe leaves for soap,' Sally said. 'Graham and I tried it one day. They make a good lather. Morag, if we go up this hill here we can see out to sea and north to the Mangamuka ranges between here and Kaitaia. It's a lovely view.'

The hill wasn't too steep, so they climbed it and

while Sally sat down, panting, with a glorious wild rose in her cheeks which hadn't been there for months, Morag gazed her fill.

'This isn't a lovely view,' she said at last. 'It's glorious —magnificent!'

Sally laughed, a little complacently, as though she held the rights to the view. 'Superb, isn't it?'

As far as the eye could see the lovely Pacific swept down the coast. Out there on that lee shore the breakers would be pounding in today; even the sheltered Bay of Islands felt an easterly. The land, a patchwork of golds and greens fading into blues and purples on the hills, dropped down towards the sea, convoluted by the forces of nature into hill and gullies and long steep ridges, wide valleys and plains and immense crags of volcanic rock.

Morag drew a deep breath and turned to the west, hoping for a glimpse of the rugged west coast, but the hills behind them were too high.

Divining her intention, Sally grinned. 'There's a lot of wild country between us and the Hokianga Harbour over there,' she said, standing up. 'Come on, Morag; time to go.'

Halfway down the slope she touched Morag's arm. 'Look, there's Thorpe, droving that mob of cattle. Sam must need exercise.'

'Sam?'

Sally chuckled. 'The horse. He's got a great long name, Abdul something, but Thorpe calls him Sam. He's a good cattle horse. Thorpe used to ride him in shows, jumping, but he got old—Sam, I mean, and Thorpe decided he had too much to do here to be able to afford the time. They look good together, don't they?'

They did indeed, the horse seeming to be an exten-

sion of the man as one beast, more stupid or more intelligent than the others, made a dash for it. Seemingly
without any signal the grey turned and within a few
seconds the steer had rejoined the herd and man and
horse had eased back into a walk.

'Thorpe's very progressive,' Sally said, 'but he likes
to stick to the old ways in some things. Horses are one.
A lot of farmers use bikes, but Thorpe says they race
the animals. Besides, there's some steep stuff here, not
suitable for bikes, though he's planted a lot of the more
slippy country into pines and allowed some of the
faces to regenerate back into native bush.'

Morag nodded, her eyes fixed on the horseman now
fairly close to them. He lifted his hand as he saw them
and came across to the fence. Sensibly, at the approach
of the mob, Morag and Sally had taken refuge in the
paddock, leaving the cattle free run of the gravelled
race which acted as a central road through the station.

In spite of this consideration, the beasts, a young and
flighty lot, evinced extreme interest in the two women
and needed the prodding of two large dogs before they
would pass the spot where Morag and Sally waited.

'Hi!' Sally laughed up at her brother's expression of
surprise. 'Morag can be very persuasive when she wants
to be.'

'Don't overdo it,' he said, but more as if he felt it
necessary to remind them than as if he was afraid they
would. 'Pleasant walking?'

'Lovely, once you get over the shock of this wind.' As
he looked at her when asking the question, Morag felt
it necessary to answer. He looked, she thought despair-
ingly, quite magnificent in gorgeous homespun jersey
knitted in an Aran pattern, and found herself wondering who had so lovingly spun the wool and then knitted
it.

An odd little prickle of emotion ran along her nerves; to hide the unpleasant sensation she shivered elaborately, saying, '*Not* the sort of weather to stand about in!'

'Not at all.' He looked aloofly at his sister. 'Do you want a lift up, Sally?'

'Oh. . . .' She looked longingly at the horse, but her innate good manners made her say, 'No, Thorpe, thank you. I'm not tired.'

But she was. The colour in her cheeks had faded and her shoulders were only held straight by a gallant effort.

Swiftly Morag said, 'Go on, be a devil. And if the children are awake, you can deal with them!'

Chuckling, Sally allowed her brother to haul her up in front of him. 'Bless you, my dear. I hadn't realised how tuckered out I am.'

'Next time we won't climb hills,' Morag called out after them as Thorpe touched his heels to the grey's sides and they moved off down the race to where the two dogs held the mob of cattle.

With a soft sigh Morag tucked her now cold hands into the pockets of her jacket and set off for the house.

A car stood on the gravel outside the front door, a big middle-aged Rolls-Royce, aristocratically aloof as only a Rolls can be. Morag looked at it with astonishment and respect as she came round the corner, planning to pay a quick visit to her favourite spot in the garden, the bush-house where Soldier's pride and joy, the cymbidiam orchids resided.

For a moment she hesitated, turning sharply when the big window into the parlour was pushed up.

'Can you come into the parlour, Morag?' Sally asked, her voice as casual as her expression was agonised. 'There's somebody here who would like to meet you.'

The somebody turned out to be two of them, Mr and Mrs Shaw, Gabrielle's parents.

And with all of their daughter's charm, Morag decided gloomily after five minutes of parrying questions she found offensively direct, though Mr Shaw was a little less arrogant than his wife. No wonder poor Sally had yelled for help! No wonder Gabrielle had about as much idea of courtesy as a rhinoceros. With a mother like this one it was a miracle she knew there was such a quality.

'And how long do you intend working for dear Sally?' Mrs Shaw demanded.

Morag lifted her brows. 'That depends on Sally,' she returned composedly.

A distinctly artificial laugh from Sally greeted this. 'I'd like to have her for ever,' she said, 'but I doubt if she'll be content to spend the next ten years looking after *my* children.'

Morag didn't know whether it was her imagination, but she had the distinct feeling that Sally was up to something. Certainly Mrs Shaw's bright blue glance flew to Morag's left hand as if searching for a ring, and there could be no doubt about the swift look both of the Shaws exchanged as if in confirmation of some doubt.

'Are you planning to marry soon?' Mrs Shaw asked with blunt offensiveness.

Morag shook her head. 'No,' she said as firmly as she could, determined not to be put into a false position once more.

Only to have it undermined immediately by Sally, who grinned and said knowingly, 'You mustn't ask such questions, dear Mrs Shaw. Morag is very deep; she prefers to present a *fait accompli*, I've discovered. Now, how is Gabrielle? I haven't seen her since I've been up. Is she away? Last time I was home she seemed to spend most of her time here.'

Mrs Shaw settled herself back into her chair, her fingers touching the opal at her lapel with something like consciousness.

'She has been away,' she admitted, speaking with a little less confidence. 'Which is really why I came to see you today, Sally. Somehow, although she asked Thorpe——' she hesitated, then went on, 'and Miss Nelson, she forgot to make sure that you had an invitation to her birthday party.' She bestowed a smile on Sally, at once gracious and acidulous. 'When I realised I knew that we had to come along immediately and rectify her mistake.'

'Which,' Sally told Morag when the Shaws were safely outside the gate, 'was a rank untruth. Ever since I queered my social pitch by marrying an impecunious scientist she's ignored me. No, she came here for quite a different reason.'

'What?'

But Sally only giggled and shook her head. 'I may not be right—although I'm almost certain I am—but I won't say, just in case I'm way off beam. Tell me, what did you think of Gabrielle?'

'Well—she's beautiful.'

'So was Mama, apparently, incredible though it may seem. What else?'

In return Morag grinned back at her. 'I hardly know the girl, so I'm not going to commit myself yet. By the way, I don't want to go to this do.'

'Then why say yes? I'm not going, but I've got a good excuse.'

'Your brother,' Morag told her grimly, 'accepted for me.'

It was amazing how sharp Sally's regard could become, uncomfortably like that same brother's. But all the older girl said was a mild, 'Well, he usually knows what he's doing. I'd trust him.'

Which was all very well, Morag mused, as she supervised the children's dinner. Sally could trust Thorpe, for she was a Cunningham, and therefore under his mantle, so to speak. Unfortunately he chose to regard Morag as a scarlet woman and apart from the bone-deep chivalry which he exhibited to all women, she was quite definitely beyond the pale. He did, of course, feel a very reluctant attraction towards her, an attraction unfortunately entirely mutual. But he had made it quite clear that he had no qualms about using her to calm Louise's absurd fears and as a shield against Gabrielle's importunities.

Not for the first time she wondered why. He was not the sort of man to need a shield. Thinking it over and remembering rather bitterly a few incidents, she could only come to the conclusion that Thorpe Cunningham was more than capable of dealing with anything that came his way. He dominated, as no one else she knew did; merely by being in a room he drew attention to himself, and it was not his build or the saturnine good looks, or even the cool command of his glance and voice. He was a natural leader, as Graham could never be. And though Morag knew much nicer men, much kinder, more thoughtful men, none of them had the physical presence which made her stupid heart thunder in her breast like a primitive drum.

Still, she thought prosaically, preventing Richie from dropping his beans on to the floor for the cat, who had a perverted taste for them; at least she was sensible enough to know that it was only physical attraction, unlike poor Gabrielle, who appeared to think herself completely head over heels in love with him. Attraction was dangerous, but it could be controlled. Morag took comfort from the fact that long ago she had been immunised by his cold ruthlessness from falling in love with him.

But she did wish that she didn't have to stay here until Sally recovered, and with all her heart she wished she didn't have to go to this party of the Shaws, where she would know no one except the Cunninghams. Judging by the parents it would be an occasion of excessive formality, probably patronised almost exclusively by people from Auckland with only a few of the locals. Even those, she thought gloomily, would be the sort of people she hadn't known when she was living in the valley. Unless she had badly misjudged them, and she was prepared to bet her mother's diamond ring that she hadn't. The Shaws were snobs. And Gabrielle would certainly not be prepared to make her unwanted guest feel at home.

Darn Thorpe Cunningham!

CHAPTER SIX

IT was a beautiful night, clear and warm, tingling with new life as the wind blew gently from the north. In the pale green western sky Venus hung like a massive silver jewel, already sinking quickly. Kopu, the Maoris called it, and in the days before calendars they had known that winter was there when it had appeared as the evening star. In a month or so it would disappear from the western sky, the Pleiades would rise in the east and summer would be truly on its way.

Better not forget that when that happened Sally's husband would be back from his icy wastes and Morag Nelson would leave the valley never to return. No one, she thought, steadfastly refusing to allow herself even a surreptitious glance at Thorpe beside her, would be happier to see the back of her than the man who was now driving her to Gabrielle Shaw's party.

Perhaps he sensed the tension she thought she had so carefully hidden, because he asked unexpectedly,

'Not jittery, are you?'

'Yes,' she answered with bald honesty.

He smiled, that rare, too attractive smile, and returned,

'You look terrific, as I've no doubt you know, and it won't really be like walking into the lion's cage. We are civilised up here.'

Defensively, for she was too aware of the potency of his charm, she said, 'I didn't want to come.'

'Scared?'

If he hoped that she would rise to the taunt in his

voice he was baffled, for she shrugged, paradoxically more at ease with him now that he was behaving true to form. 'No, not like that. I can think of better things to do than protect you from the unwanted advances of an eighteen-year-old beauty, however.'

This time he chuckled, as he retorted promptly, 'I can't. In five years' time, when she's got over being a spoilt little madam, she'll be quite a lass, but I've suffered enough embarrassment at her hands to make me wary.'

'And yet,' Morag ventured slyly, 'I'd have thought that you were more than capable of looking after yourself.'

He slanted her a swift sideways glance, mocking yet oddly intimate, as if inviting her to relax, just for this once. 'Like all men I have an inbuilt aversion to scenes,' he said primly.

Morag laughed, unable to help herself. In the warm dim confines of the car her laugh was soft and oddly beguiling, young and untouched. 'Oh, come off it,' she scoffed lightly, aware that something was happening, some strange alchemy which she had no intention of resisting. 'You eat little girls like that for breakfast.'

'I'm fond of her,' he explained. 'In spite of her rudeness and her foibles, she can be very charming. And I have a great affection for her father. It exasperates me to see her mother ruining her.'

There could be no doubt of his sincerity. Morag looked curiously at him, then asked consideringly, 'Why not take her in hand, Thorpe? She's beautiful and I've no doubt you'd lick her into shape soon enough.'

Her daring should have brought her a cutting reproof, but instead he lifted his shoulders slightly and answered readily enough. 'One reason, Miss Audacity. I said that I'm fond of her. I don't love her. And I've always felt that love is a prerequisite to marriage.'

'Truly?'

'Yes, truly.' He smiled again, a sardonic movement of his lips which was not unkind. 'That shocks you, doesn't it?'

'Well—yes,' she said slowly. 'I'd have expected you to be a cynic.'

'Oh, I am. But not entirely. You see, I had the advantage of growing up with parents who were devoted to each other, so I know it does exist. Just as Sally would accept nobody but her Sandy. I think it's an odd relationship, but it works for them. Graham, too. I think he's probably happier being unhappy with Louise than he would be without her.'

Morag moved uneasily, her fingers tightening on the clasp of her bag. Had he tossed Graham and Louise in to see how she would react? It seemed that even in rare moments of intimacy like this he could not resist jibing at her supposed misdemeanours.

'You're probably right,' she said coolly.

'I am. How about you?'

'Me? Oh—I see. Well ...' She thought and then resumed with a seriousness which made her forehead wrinkle slightly. 'Yes, I've seen some very happy marriages. And the reverse. But it's always seemed to me that friendship had a big part to play in the happiest marriages.'

'Passion dies, but a friend is a friend for ever?'

Smiling at the teasing note in his voice, she replied, 'Yes. Only I don't think passion dies, rather sort of settles down. At least, so I've heard.'

He laughed outright at that, swerving slightly to avoid a pothole. While they had been talking it had darkened completely, and the stars had sprung to life in the sky. The headlights dipped and swayed, catching now the black and white forms of someone's dairy herd, now a patch of bush, the totara and puriri trees at home in this landscape as no other tree, however beautiful, could be. Along the side of the cuttings the kumarahoe bloomed, soft gold and honey-scented, revelling in the poorest soil. Some distance ahead lay the Shaws' homestead. Stifling a sigh, Morag hoped that it was a long distance ahead.

'Is that why you've not married?' Thorpe asked as if he had every right to know. 'No friend great enough?'

'No, not exactly.' Ruefully Morag contemplated the fact that he had unerringly shown her the weak spot in her argument. Over the years she had made some very good male friends, none of whom would she dream of marrying.

He knew too, for there was amusement in his deep tones as he probed, 'Have you not fallen in love, then?'

'Several times,' she said frivolously. 'But not, alas, for any length of time. How about you?'

His retort was smooth enough, but buried deep within was a rawness which warned Morag that she trod on forbidden ground. 'Falling in love doesn't come as easily to me as to you, apparently.'

You started it, she thought indignantly, angry with herself for allowing herself to be beguiled into an intimacy which only existed for as long as he wished it. With determination she turned her head to look out of the car window while her fingers consciously relaxed on the clasp of her bag. Thorpe Cunningham was as prickly as a hedgehog, and it was wise not to forget it.

Although he lapsed into silence which lasted until they swung off the road between tall stone gateposts, once they got to the homestead he seemed to relax once more.

It was a strange evening. Morag couldn't help but be conscious of the interest in everyone's eyes and, womanlike, was glad that the clothes that she wore were every bit as sophisticated as the others', even if they weren't as expensive. She knew that the blue-green of her dress deepened the colour of her eyes and repeated the colour of Thorpe's, so that in a subtle way they became linked. And the soft, sweeping lines emphasised her figure, giving it a dignity which her height lacked.

Yes, she was well pleased with her appearance and that of her escort, almost too handsome in his evening clothes, and yes, she couldn't help being gratified by the appreciation in people's eyes when they saw them together. But she hated being the centre of attention, hated the way Thorpe made it patently clear that he was definitely the man in possession and hated the raw misery which no amount of laughter and determined flirting could banish from Gabrielle Shaw's vivid blue eyes.

In spite of all her fears it was not a terribly formal affair. Someone must have persuaded the Shaws that such a party would have been out of place, for they had hired a band which played pleasant middle-of-the-road music in a big room at the back of the house, and in other rooms there were cards and places to sit and talk, small bars and only a few waiters. Still, Morag thought, it was a far more ostentatious party than any other she had attended in a private home. And in spite of the voice within her which told her that she should be enjoying such an experience she found time dragging.

Thorpe seemed content to talk, introducing her with meticulous politeness to these people who were his friends, parrying their arch or interested questions with urbane suavity and disengaging them both when the courtesies had been observed. At last, when Morag felt that if she had to speak to another beautifully gowned and coiffured woman with avid interest written all over her exquisitely made-up face she, Morag Nelson, was going to disgrace herself by giving her well-known imitation of a bullocky urging his bullocks on, Thorpe said curtly, 'Let's dance.'

Naturally he was as competent on the dance floor as he was off it. Nothing flashy or theatrical, she thought hollowly as his hand supported her back like an iron bar, but he knew just what he wanted his partner to do and he made sure she did it.

'You dance beautifully,' he said aloofly.

'Thank you.'

After a moment he said half under his breath, 'Do you think you could bear to take that bored-to-the-bones look from your face for a few moments? It's extremely discourteous to the Shaws.'

Sheer shock robbed her of speech for a moment, but the glance she lifted to meet the cold implacability of his was glittering with anger and a hurt too deep for expression. Stiffly she said, 'I'm sorry.'

'At least *pretend* to enjoy yourself,' he went on savagely. 'Otherwise the whole idea of this masquerade is shot to pieces.'

She pinned a smile of languishing sickliness to her mouth and said, 'And we can't have that, can we? Quite frankly, Thorpe, I couldn't care less. I don't like hurting Gabrielle and as Graham and Louise aren't here——'

'Oh, but they are,' he ground out. 'And watching us.'

'So is everyone else,' she snapped. 'Wondering what the hell you see in me, I suppose!'

His smile gleamed, a light flickering in his eyes which

at once frightened and thrilled her. Without appearing to he pulled her closer against him and said softly into her ear, 'They can all see what I see in you, Morag. You've taken good care that they should, haven't you? A pretty voice, a pretty face and a very desirable body.'

His hard strength against her excited her, yet repelled her too. With a sudden darkening of her eyes she retorted, '*Don't!* I hate being—being made conspicuous.'

'Rubbish. If that's so you wouldn't be wearing a dress like that,' he said crisply. 'Now, will you play up, or do I make you more conspicuous?'

'I hate you!'

'I'm not all that sold on you, either.' With deliberate insolence he ran his hand across the delicate bowl of her hips and up her back, smiling with narrowed eyes into her face. 'You appeal to the worst in me.'

'I thought you were perfect!' she retorted, heavily sarcastic.

A muscle flicked in his jaw.

'No, I'm not perfect, but unlike you I'm honest. I've not denied my affairs. Merely been discreet.'

'Oh!' The colour rushed to her cheeks as she jutted her jaw at him, hurt and disillusioned. Goaded by anger, she snapped, 'You make me sick!'

'I doubt it.' That strange gleam came back into his expression, as he fixed her with a glance so intent it seemed to pierce through the defences she had so carefully erected against him, see right into her heart and mind. As her stomach and backbone jumped he continued, drawling, 'You should really be thankful, you know. If it weren't for this old-fashioned double standard I'd have made proper love to you long before this. But as you're a guest in my house ...'

With an immense effort Morag controlled her first,

burning instinct to tell him exactly what she thought of
him, and even managed to control her second instinctive remark, which would have been to remind him
that she, too, would have had some say in who made
love to whom! Perhaps because she was not sure of
her ground there, she bit her lip, observing defiantly,
'I hope that when you get married it will be to someone who leads you a *terrible* dance!'

The cynical amusement vanished as if her words had
conjured up a demon. 'No doubt,' he said without expression. 'But you're the one who thinks I can cope
with anything. Doesn't that apply to any prospective
wife?'

'There must be someone, somewhere, who can stand
up to you.'

'I'm dancing with her.'

Which was an astonishing admission, astonishing
enough to make Morag's glance fly upward to meet his
bland uncommunicative regard. But he had won the
exchange, if only because he left her with no way of
replying.

Later she danced with the young man who had been
Gabrielle's most constant partner, obviously a put-up
job so that poor Gabrielle would be asked by Thorpe.

The young man, whose name was Roger somebody,
was disconsolate at being coaxed into dancing with
Morag, and much to her secret amusement manoeuvred
her so that he could keep his eye on Gabrielle,

After several attempts at conversation, and failing to
make sense of his answers, Morag decided that he was
not a person who could do more than one thing at
once. After a couple of turns on the floor her toes told
her that he certainly wasn't concentrating on dancing.

'Look,' she said calmly, 'he can't rape her on the
dance floor, you know.'

'I *beg* your pardon?'

But she had caught his attention, even if his glance was intense with disapproval. 'Well,' she went on, infusing sweet reason into every note of her voice, 'I don't mind your not talking, but I do object to being trodden all over. I can assure you that Thorpe has no intention of abducting her.'

'Sorry,' he muttered, and went brilliant scarlet.

Morag felt profoundly sorry for him. 'Don't get upset,' she returned kindly. He couldn't have been much younger than her, but she felt like an elderly maiden aunt delivering strictures on the behaviour of modern youth.

After a moment he relaxed, smiling rather shamefacedly. 'I suppose you think I'm a complete fool.'

'No, not in the least. But acting like a watchdog isn't going to endear you to her, you know. Few women like jealousy.'

Casting a surreptitious look in the direction of Gabrielle and Thorpe, he said quietly, 'I suppose not, but I happen to know that——' he stopped, apparently concluding that what he had been about to say could hardly be called tactful. 'I mean,' he blundered on, 'well, Gabrielle thinks that—oh, *hell*!'

Impossible not to take pity on him. Morag smiled, mischief making her roguish. 'I know that she has a crush on Thorpe,' she told him serenely.

He looked his relief, his pleasant face relaxing into a smile which disappeared as soon as it had come. 'Doesn't it worry you?'

'No, not in the least.' Then, remembering that she was supposed to be Thorpe's latest girl-friend and that such calmness was hardly in keeping with someone who could be expected to feel at least a tiny bit of love for him, she added, 'She's very young, much too young for Thorpe.'

'She's very beautiful.'

Morag chuckled and he flushed again.

'No, don't get so uptight,' she said, before he could voice his confusion. 'Of course she is, but surely you don't admire her for her beauty alone? No, I thought as much,' as he shook his head. 'So why think that of Thorpe? They have nothing else in common, and whatever you've heard, he's not the sort to run after every lovely woman he sees.'

Heavens, but he was young! Another flush touched his skin, but he said manfully, 'You should know, I guess, but he has a bit of a reputation. And I think Gabrielle really believes that she's in love with him.'

'She'll get over it,' Morag told him prosaically. 'Calf love is fierce, but it feeds on itself and collapses quickly. Give her time.'

Eminently sensible advice, which made it unfortunate that she should at that exact moment lift her eyes to see Thorpe and Gabrielle, he smiling down into her rapt face with all of his formidable charm only too apparent. Morag missed a step as a pang of some totally unknown emotion seared through her and she found herself wishing that once, just once—he would look at her like that, as if he found her the most fascinating woman he had known.

Fortunately at that moment the music stopped, and she found herself in a group which contained Graham and Louise as well as Gabrielle. And although she fumed when Thorpe tucked his arm around her waist and pulled her back to rest against him, making his proprietorial claim obvious, she felt a warmth kindling deep inside her which had little to do with his physical nearness.

After that the evening assumed an unreal air. Mindful of Thorpe's strictures on the dance floor, she set out to be, if not brilliant and witty, at least interested and interesting.

As the initial stiffness of the occasion had well worn off by this time and everyone was fully prepared to enjoy themselves this was not difficult, and she began to relax into her normal self. In fact, if it had not been for Thorpe, ever-present, making her far too conscious of him, she would have thoroughly enjoyed herself, for over the years she had gained enough poise and social expertise to play this sort of game with ease and confidence.

Once or twice she found herself wondering whether people would have been so flatteringly interested if she had not been there with Thorpe, but she knew that she was not dull and dismissed such a thought without troubling herself overmuch about it.

It was while they were at supper, just after the champagne toast to the birthday girl, that someone tapped Morag on the shoulder, saying diffidently, 'Morag? Morag Nelson?'

Turning, she gave an exclamation of surprise. 'Why, *Greg*! How lovely to see you!'

He grinned and kissed her upturned forehead, dark eyes twinkling with amusement as Thorpe looked him over.

For a moment something ugly showed in that steady, almost insolent gaze. Morag felt as though a freezing wind blew about her and with less than her usual confidence made the introduction.

'Greg Layton is an old friend,' she told him somewhat lamely, recalling too clearly Thorpe's suspicions of her morals.

'Oh, darling, how tactful!' Greg was at his most infuriating, his eyes dancing with laughter, his twisted grin very much in evidence. 'I loved you madly for three months while you looked after my sister's baby and turned your cold cheek to me.'

'Exaggerating, as usual.' Morag, refusing to be intimidated by Thorpe's aloofness, met his eyes with defiance. 'Greg and I met in the Mackenzie country, on his brother-in-law's station.'

'Miles from anywhere,' Greg supplied cheerfully. 'I had to have a nice dry climate—my chest had been playing me up.'

'How is it?'

'Oh, fine, thanks.' He smiled, every bit as charming as Thorpe could be, and continued, 'I couldn't believe my eyes when I saw you, sweet. What are you doing here?'

'Deciding whether she could bear to live here for the rest of her life,' Thorpe astonishingly interjected.

Not to be outdone in the charm line, he took Morag's hand, holding it loosely but possessively, and used his superior height to dwarf Greg.

Always quick on the uptake, Greg looked across to Morag's astounded face and smiled wryly. 'How nice for Morag. A very pretty place, this neck of the woods, I always think; but I don't know that I'd like to spend the rest of my life here. Too far from the bright lights.'

By this time Morag had regained most of her composure, although Thorpe's hand around hers was warningly tight, daring her to deny the implication of his words. Trying to bring some semblance of normality into the conversation, she said swiftly, 'Rubbish! You loved the Mackenzie country.'

'Ah, that's a bit different, isn't it? The air is so incredibly clear and pure, the tussocks tawny-gold—it's a different world.' Greg shrugged before saying carelessly, 'There are some Cunninghams down there on Flathead station.'

'My cousin,' Thorpe supplied.

Greg nodded. 'I thought he had a look of you.'

The conversation became general, a free-ranging discussion of people and places over the country, in which Greg and Thorpe found that they had many friends, or friends of friends, in common; they discussed farming practices and from thence drifted into current affairs, which was more up Morag's alley. She and Greg had argued amiably for hours sometimes, so he was surprised at her contributions, but she felt Thorpe's glance on her and once, after commenting, heard the surprise in his voice as he took her up on a point.

It made her angry with a deep cold anger which lent a glitter to her glance and an unconscious firmness to her tones. How stupid she had been to feel that she could perhaps be endangered by her foolish heart and fall in love with Thorpe! He was unknown to her; she had thought that she understood him, but listening to him talk just now had taught her that she knew only one side of him, the side he kept no doubt for his mistresses, she thought, pushing the dagger home. It took another man to bring that keen incisive mind into play. Intuitively she recognised that he would be a superb lover, but she would need more than that from the man she loved. True companionship was perhaps rarer than passion but every bit as worthwhile, and it seemed that Thorpe sought friendship from men, keeping women firmly in their place.

Unless—horrid thought, she had behaved so stupidly with him that he considered her a complete mental lightweight!

This toned down her anger somewhat, but the embers of it were still burning when at last they left for home. Behind them the homestead lights shone bravely, for many people were still there, determined to see the night out, but when Thorpe had lifted his brows at Morag she had nodded. Somehow she had lost the desire for gaiety.

There had been an awkward few moments when Gabrielle pleaded with them to stay, but Thorpe had smoothed that over and soon they were back in the car. It was very late and Morag was tired, so tired that even the unexpected coldness of the air couldn't keep her awake. Thorpe switched on the heater and slowly her head slid sideways as her lashes were dragged downwards.

'Wake up!' His voice was impatient but amused, a dark cord of sound in the quietness of the car.

Morag groaned. 'Oh! Are we home?'

'Home? Yes, we're back.' She could tell that he was smiling, when he asked, 'Do you want me to carry you in?'

This brought her awake as nothing else could have. 'No, I'm quite capable of walking.'

'O.K. Out you get.' He leaned across and opened the door and the interior light sprang on, illuminating the dark authority of his features.

Instinctively Morag pressed herself back against the seat, receiving a glance of sardonic amusement. But beyond murmuring again, 'Out you get,' he said nothing, leaving her to make her way out of the car and into the pitch blackness of the garage. This had been built on to the house, probably at the time that the place had been renovated, and designed with a considerable amount of skill so that it did not look out of place. A door to one side led to the passage; unfortunately Morag couldn't work out where the door or the light switch were and as the lights in the car were out she could not see a thing.

So she stood there, unmoving, listening as Thorpe came around the car towards her.

'You must have eyes like a cat,' she said after a moment.

'Can't you see? Here, take my hand.'

There wasn't much else she could do, but she shivered slightly as he drew her along behind him.

'You're cold.'

'It's cold in here.'

'Thank God for central heating!'

The door clicked, the light in the house gleamed and then they were inside and the lovely warmth enclosed Morag, so that she felt tireder than ever.

'Better?'

'Oh yes,' she said, wondering how she was going to get her hand away from him.

He solved the problem by drawing her towards him, smiling in a set fashion which warned her that she had better not resist his determination to kiss her goodnight.

But she didn't have to enjoy it, she thought angrily, as his mouth descended on hers with a strength which was more like brutality. He did not want her to enjoy it; she felt that he was purging himself of desires which she had not provoked, and against her instincts began to struggle, shamed and angered by his harshness.

'Not your usual reaction,' he taunted, holding her effortlessly still.

'You're just using me.'

He laughed softly, a sound without any humour in it. 'If I wanted to use you, as you so tritely put it, I'd have you in my bed, not in my arms. Why this sudden prudishness?'

From between her bruised lips she said stonily, 'I don't like being kissed as if I were a—a thing! Let me go, Thorpe. You don't need anything else from me. No one can see us now to be affected by this farce. Let me go!'

The sea-green sharpness of his glance became a steely glitter, so piercing that she had the greatest difficulty meeting it. Like that he reminded her of an eagle, fierce, cruel, predatory, caring nothing for anything but the satisfaction of his needs.

'I suppose Greg Layton's arrival on the scene wouldn't have anything to do with this unusual girlishness?' he asked coolly.

Morag gaped, then, as the implication struck her, angrily retorted, 'No! There was never anything between Greg and me. Thorpe, it's late—and I'm tired—and although you seem to think that you can maul me whenever the fancy takes you it's quite unnecessary. And unwelcome. I want to go to bed.'

'Then go,' he ground out harshly.

'How can I, when you're holding me as if I were a—a greasy pig!'

To her astonishment he flung back his head and laughed, laughed as if to clear all of his anger and desire away, and when she looked uncertainly up at him, bent and kissed her with what seemed to be tenderness. 'Go on, Morag, get off to bed. But I want to see you after breakfast in the study.'

Bemused, she made her way up to her bedroom, and lay long awake listening for him to come up. To no avail.

CHAPTER SEVEN

COLD night gave way to an idyllic morning, soft and warm and clear, without a trace of the blueing haze which was always a sign of summer's imminence up here in the north. Out on the terrace it was almost as warm as summer, Morag thought, lifting her face to the sun; the bees thought so too, as they hummed vigorously among the white and lilac froth of the alyssum blossom. A native pigeon flew clumsily overhead, its white breast gleaming like a boiled shirt amid the iridescent bronze-green of its plumage. It was followed by two parakeets, glittering gaudy missiles in their scarlet and blue and yellow, cheeky thieves in the orchard but so beautiful that few harmed them.

From where she stood Morag could see the white bridal veil of the native clematis over several tall trees in the little patch of native bush beyond the garden, and she felt that pleasure which is so closely akin to pain that it is impossible to separate them. Wharuaroa was beautiful, never more so than in the spring, she thought dreamily, then, as though she had fallen headlong into a trap, she reminded herself hastily of other places which were beautiful too, where spring was no gentle continuation of a mild winter but a triumphal shout of praise and exultation after the bleakness of snow and cold.

It seemed as though the sun had magnetic powers, for although it was early she heard the noise of the door behind her opening, and turning saw Thorpe coming towards her.

Her smile was hesitant. 'Good morning.'

'Good morning.' Without embarrassment he stretched and yawned.

Watching the play of muscles as they rippled beneath his shirt, Morag thought that he was a splendid animal, superbly fit and with the co-ordination that came from perfect health. Then her glance was caught by his, and at the glint of amusement in the sea-coloured depths she flushed, and turned back into the house.

'Don't go,' he ordered swiftly, catching her by the shoulder. 'I've something I want to discuss with you.'

'Here?'

'Well, we could go for a walk. Come and see the orchids.'

The orchids had their own bush-house, sheltered from the wind and the sun. Morag loved them, the great arcs of flowers like butterflies, the green sword-like leaves, but she felt that their home was far too enclosed for any discussion with Thorpe. Intimacy was the one thing she did not want, since it set her at a complete disadvantage.

However, at her hesitation his jaw had hardened in that particularly forbidding fashion which was his alone, and she did not feel like spoiling the pleasure of the morning by fighting with him, so contenting herself with a slight shrug, she allowed him to lead her across the dew-wet lawn. And deep inside, some perverse part of her mind was happy that she was wearing an elegantly cut pair of trousers and a thin blue shirt which emphasised the slender lines of her body.

Once there Thorpe seemed to have forgotten his purpose in bringing them that far, apparently quite content to follow her around as she exclaimed with delight. Thereby revealing another facet of the man, for when he touched the blooms his hands were as deft and gentle as a woman's; it was clear that he too found them beautiful. But you'd expect a farmer to have gentle hands, she thought, for he dealt with animals, many of them sick. Thorpe had trained as a veterinarian and coped with all the casualties at Wharuaroa.

Uneasily she moved ahead, aware that her emotions towards him were undergoing some sort of change, and knowing, too, that although she didn't approve of what was happening she seemed powerless to prevent it. When he spoke she jumped, absurdly nervous, turning to face him with something close to defiance deepening the blue of her eyes to almost black.

'Relax,' he said, looking grimly amused. 'I'm not going to hit you.'

'You look as if you could!'

He smiled, without the amusement this time. 'Rubbish. And don't try to pretend you're afraid of me, because I know damned well that you're not.'

'Very well then, I won't. But would you mind telling me what all this is about? I mean, it's rather cloak-and-daggerish. What are you up to?'

She spoke nonsense because the sound of her own voice gave her courage of a sort, but was not surprised when he frowned.

'Chicanery—or to put it more bluntly, misrepresentation. Yesterday Graham said something to me which made me think that Louise has been rude to you.'

What *now*! Morag eyed him warily but said nothing.

'Well, is this so?' he persisted.

'If it is, what has it to do with you? I'm quite capable of looking after myself.'

He frowned, more heavily this time, his lean face darkened with anger and pride. 'I know that. Look,' speaking as if he had made up his mind about something, 'I don't know if you're aware of the set-up here, but knowing that chatterbox of a sister of mine, I'd guess that you've a pretty good idea of how the station was left.'

Startled, Morag nodded. It must go against the grain for him to discuss his personal affairs with her, but she could not prevent a tiny warm glow at the thought that he trusted her even if only a little bit.

'Yes,' she said when it was clear he wanted an answer. 'I know it was left to you—outright.'

'And that Graham, perhaps understandably, feels that he was deprived of his birthright?'

'Yes.'

'That he wants the station divided?'

'Yes.' She looked at him directly. 'Would that be such a crime?'

His answer was a twisted smile. 'Unfortunately Graham hasn't changed over the years. He would enjoy himself by doing all the things I've refused to allow him to do. One of the first being that the bush on the hills would be cut and pines planted in their place.'

'Oh *no*!' If he had looked for a way to enlist her sympathy he could not have chosen a better. Morag knew that pines were an important part of the country's economy, but to deliberately cut down the magnificent stands of primeval forest, some of it unaltered for the last five hundred years, would be a sin. And she could believe that Graham would do it. After his behaviour in telling lies about their relationship she knew he could not be trusted.

'Oh yes.' Thorpe paused, as though unsure whether to tell her more, then went on slowly, 'I've been trying to persuade him to move on to a fat stock place we own in the Waikato, but he seems to feel that to leave

Wharuaroa would be to lose a battle. The only person who could make him go is Louise. But Louise likes the advantages, social and financial, of being a Cunningham of Wharuaroa.'

Morag bit her lip as a suspicion of what he had in mind surfaced. 'So——'

'Has she been rude to you?'

'Yes.'

He nodded. 'Louise being Louise, if we become engaged, she'll leave. She couldn't bear the thought of you queening it over her.'

Morag repressed a shiver of—anguish? Surely not! Then she sat down on a conveniently placed box, marshalled her energies and retorted crisply, 'Look, you've a colossal nerve even to suggest such an idea! To begin with, I've only your word that Louise will decide to go. How do you know that she won't decide it's much more fun to stay here and make my life a misery?'

He shrugged. 'I know her.' Then with barely repressed violence, 'God knows, I've had enough time to get to know her.'

'Yes—well, I suppose so.' Morag blinked, nervously aware that he was beginning to intimidate her as he had done before when first he had mooted the idea of this wretched entanglement. Into her mind popped Sally's dark insinuation. What *was* it she had said about Louise? Something about Louise spending her time fretting because she had married the wrong brother. A fleeting glance at Thorpe's dark countenance made her wonder if perhaps Louise had tried to do something about that.

'Oh, *really*!' she exclaimed, horrified at her thoughts. How appalling to sink low enough to surmise such horrible things about Louise!

With a swift movement she sprang to her feet, in-

tending to put as much distance as possible between
herself and Thorpe before he could browbeat her into
a fake engagement. But once more reading her mind
he swung her round even as she moved, his fingers hard
on her upper arm, keeping her still so that he could
survey her angry, mutinous expression.

Oddly enough he didn't begin to threaten. 'I'm
sorry it should be so distasteful to you,' he began, his
lip curling as if he thought of her response to his lovemaking, 'but believe me, Morag, it is important.'

'Yes, but—oh, Thorpe, I hate living a lie as it is. And
this—this will be so much worse a one. Sally . . .'

'Sally?' He shook her slightly. 'If it makes you feel
any happier I'll tell Sally the truth.'

Her eyes searched his face, willing him to show some
tiny chink in that incredible armour of his, but to no
avail. It didn't seem fair, she thought desperately, that
so handsome a man should be so implacable, so hard to
resist.

As if he knew that she was almost ready to give in he
said gently, 'It will make things easier for Sally, too.
I'm sure I don't have to tell you that she doesn't like
Louise. And Morag——'

'Yes?'

'—believe me when I say that I think it will be for
Louise and Graham's ultimate benefit, too. Once
Graham gets away from here and becomes his own man,
the canker of envy and frustration will stop eating into
him and he'll be much happier.'

'And Louise?'

He shrugged, holding her glance. 'She loves him,
whether you believe it or not. Once she realises that
he's happy she'll have a better chance of happiness herself.'

'I hope you're right,' she sighed, defeated by his inexorable logic—and by a traitor within which had become a part of her so insidiously that she was scarcely aware of it.

'I am,' he returned inflexibly, releasing her with that air of hauteur which angered her so much.

Feeling rather as if she had been run over by a steamroller Morag stood her ground, saying steadily, 'And that doesn't give you the right to maul me whenever you feel like it!'

'No?' He dropped a careless arm about her shoulders, continuing with a nasty note of sarcasm in his deep voice, 'Relax. It will be a purely business arrangement, except for those moments when it's considered necessary for me to—er—maul you ... in the interests of veracity.'

'Just so that you know!' she retorted belligerently, angry that she should feel such a sense of security at his touch.

They walked back to the house through the smiling morning, and if the colours seemed brighter and the sun warmer than before, Morag had only the faintest suspicion of the reason for it. As they came up the steps on to the terrace she saw them for a moment reflected in the glass of the door, Thorpe towering over her by a head, moving with the easy athlete's stride, and she, small and slim, with her shoulders straight beneath his arm, her hair dark against the green of his sleeve, almost insignificant against him.

Sally met them, grinning, her eyes dancing beneath her red curls. 'Just getting home?' she enquired slyly, and burst out laughing.

'I'm too old for all-night jinks,' Thorpe told her. 'Behave yourself, Sally. Morag has just agreed to marry me.'

Morag sent him an astonished glance, her head reeling with shock. Surely he should have told Sally of the facts before springing such an announcement on her?

But she had to content herself with a speaking glance at him, one he met with a blandness she found intensely irritating, before Sally squealed with joy. That brought out Hazel and Soldier and the boys, and in the welter of congratulations, hugs and kisses, Morag's spirits sank to rock-bottom. She hated lying to these people she had grown so fond of, and when Sally told the boys that they must learn to call her Aunt Morag, she could not prevent a direct appeal to Thorpe.

'Didn't you say you had something to discuss with Sally?' she asked, her clear voice almost sharp with repressed emotion.

He had appeared to be enjoying the fuss, smiling for all the world as if today was the happiest day of his life. Not that he revealed overmuch, he had too much reserve to wear his emotions like flags, but he didn't need to unbend quite so much, Morag thought angrily, wondering why she felt as if she would burst into tears if anyone else wished her happiness.

Sally was only away with him for ten minutes. When she came back to the kitchen Morag was trying to persuade the excited boys to eat their porridge. Sally chuckled, apparently not in the least subdued by Thorpe's revelation of the true state of affairs.

'Thorpe wants to see you,' she said. 'You *are* sly ones, aren't you?'

And that was that. Morag stared, but when Sally repeated, 'Thorpe wants you, love,' she left her and made her way to his study.

It was a room she hadn't been in before, a somewhat sombre chamber lined with books. A framed map of the station took pride of place on one wall; behind the desk there were paintings of impossibly fat cattle on the panelled wall. Eighteenth century, Morag thought; they were quaint, giving the room something of the air of an English study, but his taste didn't run to hunting scenes. Instead there were two beautiful landscapes, starkly typical of the New Zealand scenery.

Thorpe was looking at boxes on the desk, jewellery boxes. Moved by some unknown impulse, Morag tucked her hands behind her back, flushing slightly as she met his ironic gaze.

'I thought you might like to wear one of these rings,' he said, faint amusement colouring his tones. 'And don't make objections. No one is going to believe that I'd refuse you a ring.'

Morag, who had been going to do just that, bit her lip.

'As a chain of servitude, I presume,' she snapped, angry because he had managed to read her mind again.

'Of course. I brand everything which belongs to me,' he agreed smoothly. 'Would you prefer a new one?'

'Oh—no!' Caught by the age-old lure of precious stones, she gazed as he opened the boxes to reveal their contents.

'They're lovely,' she said quietly after a long moment, her eyes caught and held by the colours. 'They have a magic.'

'Yes. The appeal of beauty.' He removed a ruby, flame caught in crystal, and slipped it on her finger. 'That was my grandmother's. Do you mind an old-fashioned setting?'

A quick look showed that he was quite serious. Morag felt a strange twist somewhere in the region of her heart at the realisation that he was prepared to risk his family jewellery with her.

Speaking more naturally than perhaps ever before in his presence she answered swiftly, 'Of course not. I'll take the greatest care.'

'Not that, I think.' He removed the ruby and slid on a sapphire, a beautiful blue the colour of tropical seas at dusk, saying with practised charm, 'It's the colour of your eyes.'

'Hardly,' she protested, but it was the one she liked best, so she let it remain there. To her small capable hand it gave an air of glamour which was odd but excitingly different. Morag had very little jewellery, except for a delicate gold chain her mother had left her, and it struck her as strange that this man, who thought of her as a common little tramp, should put such an exquisite gem on her finger.

It flashed, deep, mysteriously alive, in a ray of sunlight. To hide her complicated emotions she said briskly, 'That's that, then. Who did this belong to?'

'An aunt.'

It seemed that he regretted his former expansiveness, for the answer to her question was curt and he followed it up by saying as if bored to screaming point with the whole subject, 'I've talked to Sally.'

'Yes, I'd gathered that.'

'Good.' He looked strangely at the slightly downbent head, then came round the desk to take her by the hands and continue with unexpected wryness, 'Don't look so forlorn. Being engaged to me isn't the end of the world. Think of it as a game, or a job, if that makes it easier.'

Impossible to tell him that this fleeting sadness was not entirely based on her objections to lying. Even as he pulled her towards him Morag discovered that she wanted to be his fiancée, that the unexpected ache in her heart was because the whole thing was a lie. She was in love with the man, had been for weeks, and had been too unaware of the tendencies of her wayward heart to know that it was being captured by his dark attraction.

In his arms she rested against him, feeling a security such as she had never known before.

The weight of his cheek on the top of her head was bliss, bliss, too, the realisation that there was no passion in his embrace, but a tenderness she valued far more than easily aroused desire.

'I suppose,' he murmured after a few moments, 'most women want romance in an engagement and feel cheated if it's not a part of the bargain. Is that why you look as if somebody has stolen your orange?'

'I don't know,' she returned, trying desperately to infuse some of her usual briskness into her tones. 'Thorpe——'

'Yes?'

'Oh, it doesn't matter.' She had been going to ask him if he still believed that she and Graham had been lovers, but she didn't want to destroy the fragile peace of the moment. And if he had not changed his mind she didn't want to know. After all, she thought ruefully, she had given him no reason to believe otherwise, responding only too ardently to him. Wantonly, in fact, possessed by something she now realised was love and the desire of that love for complete union with the loved one.

He said, sounding as if he was smiling, 'You're a comfortable thing to cuddle, Morag, but I have work to do. Before you go, however, I'd better have a few details from you for the engagement notice.'

'The notice?' She stiffened, pulling away so that she could see into the lean inflexibility of his features.

'Yes. Like the ring, if there's no notice it lacks that air of verisimilitude.'

She smiled, but absently, at the quotation before saying, 'Oh dear, that—I hadn't thought of that.'

'Think of it now,' he told her crisply. 'I'll want your parents' names.'

Somewhat snappily she told him, chilled by his abrupt changes of mood, and watched as he wrote them down.

Then, as she turned to go, he said without expression, 'I think we should call a truce, you and I, until this is all over.'

Warily she nodded, wondering exactly what calling a truce implied, and more than ever determined to allow him no opportunities to penetrate the hidden defences of her heart. That would really amuse him, to discover that the girl he so despised had fallen in love with him!

'So docile?' he asked with unexpected amusement. 'I expected to have my offer thrown in my teeth.'

A faint flush touched her cheeks, but she answered steadily, 'You can hardly blame me for being prickly with you.'

'No, I don't. Not in the least. Well, that's settled. All you have to do now is act as convincingly as you can, so that Louise is fooled.'

Morag could not prevent herself from returning with a crispness to match his, 'Don't you mean *we* have to act?'

'I have no doubts about my own ability,' he said, smiling very beguilingly. 'Whereas you, my black-haired vixen, are only too likely to lose your temper with me and spoil the whole show.'

'I won't,' she said, breathlessly, and made good her

escape as her heart beat an alarming one-two in her breast. Thorpe was altogether too much, and he knew it, she reflected crossly.

And the first person she ran into was Richie, who was practising saying, 'Aunty Morag, Aunty Morag,' over and over again as he ran one of his fleet of Matchbox toys along the borders of the Persian rug in the hall. He gave her a wide and charming smile and said proudly, 'I can remember to say Auntie, Morag, but Jason can't. He still calls you Morag by itself.'

In the sudden release from tension Morag laughed, bent to hug him fiercely, and said, 'You're *both* very clever, my boy. Where's Mummy?'

'Upstairs with Jason and Rachel.'

They were all in the nursery, Rachel cooing and talking as she rolled over on the floor, Jason 'helping' to make a bed.

'What's this, then?' Morag asked in surprise as she came through the door. 'Sally, you're not supposed to be exerting yourself.'

'But Jason is helping me,' Sally pleaded, looking mischievous. 'And I'm sick to death of lying about. Truly, Morag, I feel one hundred per cent better. I think it must be spring.'

'One fine day?' Morag scoffed, stripping the other bed with the ease of long practice.

'Oh, more than that, I think. It *feels* like a new season. Any day now we'll be hearing the shining cuckoo and we'll know that summer is nearly here.'

'The shining cuckoo probably hasn't even thought of leaving its tropical islands for the long trip back here,' Morag retorted, but added, 'It *is* a beautiful day. I know we'll have rain and cold days again, but you're right, it does feel as though winter is past.'

'Well, yours is, anyway,' said Sally. 'From now on, my dear, you behave as a member of the family, not as my children's nurse.'

Morag looked across the narrow width of the bed, surprised at the purposeful note in her companion's light voice. 'I can be both, surely,' she objected.

'We'll share and share alike as far as the children are concerned. No, I mean it,' as Morag began to protest. 'Thorpe will want to show you off and he won't like it if that over-developed sense of duty prevents you from going out with him. As a matter of fact he and I have decided to have a small party in a few days' time to introduce you to his very closest friends. And you're going to enjoy it!'

If her determination could have produced such a result there was no doubt that Sally would have forced Morag to revel in the situation, but torn between her shame at the deception and the pain of finding out just how deeply she had taken Thorpe into her heart, Morag found herself becoming wary and defensive.

When during the afternoon, Lauren rang up to invite her to dinner she had to say sadly, 'I'm sorry, Lauren, but I can't come. I'll be busy up here.'

'Oh, poor old thing. Never mind, some other time. Or—tell you what, why don't you come down this afternoon and have a cup of coffee with me? Bring the boys.'

Morag frowned, then gasped as the receiver was taken from her hand. 'Hey!' she exclaimed, but Thorpe said, holding his hand over the mouthpiece so that Lauren couldn't hear, 'When does she want you to come?'

'This afternoon.'

Speaking into the receiver, he said coolly, 'Thorpe

here, Lauren. I'll bring her down round about three-ish. How's that?'

The little voice at the other end said something. Thorpe shook his head. 'Sorry, we're tied up tonight; but this afternoon will be fine. See you then.'

Morag smouldered, but before she could demand to know why he assumed the right to make arrangements for her he said with his infuriating brand of assurance, 'She'll have to know before the actual notice comes out, as she and Alan are old friends.'

Morag nodded, seeing the logic of that, but asked, 'What about tonight?'

'Tonight we have Graham and Louise up, to drink our health. I've just invited them.'

'Oh—murder!'

'I hope not,' he said, grimly amused at the childish exclamation, 'but it's probably just as well that they've got the whole day to mull over the news. I decided it wouldn't be a terribly good idea to spring it on them tonight.'

'No, indeed,' Morag agreed fervently, recalling Louise's unbalanced method of expressing herself.

'Scared?' he taunted with a return of the mockery she found so hard to cope with.

'No. Uneasy, but not scared.'

'Well, that's all right then. Come and have lunch before Hazel beats the brass off that gong.'

Wharuaroa was the only place where Morag had ever lived where the meals were signalled in the time-honoured fashion. Now she smiled, saying, 'I'm afraid that's probably Richie. The thing holds a fatal fascination for him, although he knows he's not permitted to touch it. Hazel lets him indulge himself at the right times.'

Lauren and her Alan lived down the valley in a smart modern house set a hundred yards or so back from the road. The drive was bordered by totara trees, their stiff olive prickles of leaf overlaid by the soft jade of the spring growth.

Looking around her with pleasure, Morag said, 'How pretty it is! But how new, compared to Wharuaroa.'

'Are you like Lauren, who wouldn't care to live in an old house?' Thorpe asked as they rattled over the traffic stop.

Morag shot him a sharp glance but answered mildly, 'No, not at all. Old homes have character; it will take years before this garden approaches the loveliness of yours.'

The drive broadened out to a cobblestoned area in front of the house where cars could park and turn. Bordered by flowers and small shrubs, it looked pretty but characterless compared to the lush beauty of Wharuaroa. Morag said as much, not really sure why she had to convince Thorpe of her preference for the mature loveliness of his home. Being in love with someone, she had discovered, meant that the least hurt to their feelings was painful.

She must have succeeded, for he grinned down at her as he opened the car door and said, 'I acquit you of a hankering for things shiny and modern, then. Come on in, before Lauren bursts with curiosity.'

Indeed, it seemed as though their hostess had been on tenterhooks, for she flung open the door before they got there, saying impetuously, 'I've been waiting *ages* for you! Do come in. Thorpe, I've made the most sumptuous sponge cake, better than anything Hazel's ever done, I'll bet.'

This was apparently a long-standing joke, for Thorpe grinned but said, 'I'll have to taste it before I can pass judgment. Morag, can you make a good sponge?' His voice was caressing, smooth and bland as the cream on the said sponge.

'No,' Morag retorted, flushing as Lauren's incredulous gaze flew to her guest's left hand, 'but I'm a dab hand at baked Alaska!'

Lauren spied the sapphire and said pleadingly, 'Tell me—please—in case I make a horrible mistake!'

'You're the first to know outside the family,' Thorpe told her. 'We became officially engaged before breakfast this morning.'

'Oh—how lovely!' Lauren kissed them both with fervour, called for Alan several times, and bustled them into a sleek modern living room, exclaiming in a way which left no doubt about her pleasure. 'Not,' she finished slyly, 'that I'm all that surprised, because the grapevine has been pretty busy, but everybody had just about given up on you, Thorpe. Alan'—as her husband came in, 'Alan, Morag and Thorpe are engaged!'

He, too, said all that was right, cracked a mild joke about the noose, smiling proudly at his vivacious wife in a way which made it quite clear that he thought marriage the greatest institution ever created.

It should have been a happy hour or so, but Morag found herself feeling wistful and had to force the appearance of relaxation and good humour which seemed to come so easily to Thorpe. The fact that she was acutely aware of him, dominant and watchful beside her, did not help at all. Smoothly, without any fuss, he used his social expertise to ensure that Lauren and Alan should suspect nothing, giving an excellent imitation of Thorpe Cunningham in love, Morag thought, stifling the ache in her heart.

Choosing her clothes with particular care, she took

much longer than normal to dress; with purely feminine instinct she was using her appearance as an armour against what she suspected was going to be a very sticky evening.

When at last she was ready, she stood for long moments staring into the mirror. Her reflection stared sombrely back at her, a slight slip of a thing, black hair outlining a face which was not pretty but arresting with the dark blue of her eyes and the well-formed, well-disciplined mouth. She had chosen a blouse in warm apricots and golds above a deep copper velvet skirt. The colours gave her skin the warmth of summer and a skilful use of blusher had hidden the pallor which seemed to have become an integral part of her complexion. So that she should not appear too dwarfed by Thorpe's height, she wore her latest extravagance, a pair of sinfully high-heeled sandals which flattered her slender feet.

Altogether very sleek and sophisticated, she thought dryly as she turned her back on the girl in the mirror. That girl could play Thorpe's game without any of the tension and pain which were beginning to rack the real Morag, making her less than she had been because the living, feeling part of her had become Thorpe's unwanted possession.

Worse than useless to wish fervently that she had never allowed herself to be pushed into this mock engagement. If she had stood out against him right from the first she might have had some chance, but he had imposed his will on her without effort, using all the methods at his disposal, from emotional blackmail to appeals to her better nature, and she had had little defence against him even at the start.

A thought struck her as she was half-way down the stairs, a thought which drew her dark brows together

in a frown and made her halt a moment. Graham
would now believe that Thorpe did not trust his ver-
sion of that long-ago affair.

And just how would that affect Graham's attitude
towards leaving Wharuaroa? Morag tried to guess at
his reactions, but he was now an unknown quantity to
her. She knew only one thing, that Thorpe, with his
cynical detachment, would have taken this into account too. He overlooked nothing.

'Half-way down the stairs is not the place to start
changing your mind,' Sally said from behind her. 'Have
you got cold feet or something? Because if you have,
forget them. Thorpe has no time for ditherers.'

'I'm not dithering,' Morag summoned up a smile as
she accompanied Sally down the stairs. 'Just thinking.'

'You'll have plenty of time for that later. For the
present I'd concentrate on Thorpe,' her companion retorted with an exaggerated leer. 'Still,' becoming
solemn almost immediately, 'it might pay to keep your
wits about you. I have a feeling that this is going to be
some evening!'

CHAPTER EIGHT

IT started pleasantly enough, although to Morag's acutely sharpened senses the tension in the room was heavy, almost threatening. In fact, the atmosphere positively crackled when Louise and Graham came in, but as they appeared to be on their best behaviour she was able to accept their felicitations with equanimity, accepting the cool pressure of Louise's cheek against hers as calmly as she inclined her face for Graham's kiss.

Suave as ever, Thorpe poured drinks while Sally, displaying a social talent which should not have surprised Morag but did, ably backed him up, so that everything ran smoothly enough, if you could except Morag's jittery pulse every time she felt Thorpe's sea-green glance on her.

Nobody could ever call Louise effusive, but she had excellent manners when she chose to use them; the evening revealed an entirely different woman from the snobbish neurotic creature that Morag had encountered before. Graham seemed subdued, his thin handsome countenance shuttered as though resisting observation, but Morag looked up several times to catch his eyes on her and immediately felt a profound disquiet.

Just before dinner Louise asked, 'And when do you plan to be married, Thorpe?'

'As soon as possible,' he said immediately.

With a conscious effort of will Morag prevented herself from showing her astonishment, for Louise was watching her closely.

'It's unlike you to be so precipitate,' Louise smiled. 'Is there a reason?'

Thorpe shrugged, but the tiny flicker of anger in his eyes was steady as he answered, 'The usual one, Louise. You must remember how you felt before you and Graham were married. And there's no reason to wait.'

'Of course not.' Louise set her glass down with deliberation. Leaning back in her chair she looked like a fairytale princess, cool and poised, her blonde hair like a crown against the rich damask of the upholstery fabric. 'It must be unusual for two brothers to love the same woman,' she remarked, making the sharp words sound like a light pleasantry.

Ignoring Graham's movement of protest, Thorpe reached his hand out to Morag, and when she took it pulled her against him, holding her steady against the hardness of his muscular side. 'I don't really think you could call that old boy–girl affair true love,' he commented, sounding amused and slightly bored. 'Certainly not as far as Morag was concerned, anyway.' He lifted a brow at her.

'No, I'm afraid it wasn't,' she managed, feeling embarrassment and relief at having things out in the open. Infusing what she hoped was the right amount of reminiscent feeling into her tones, she looked directly at Graham, and smiled, 'And nothing so world-shattering for you, I know.'

He tossed her an angry, taken-aback glance. Then his eyes shifted to Thorpe's, were held there for a long moment and dropped. 'Well, it's a long time ago,' he said reluctantly.

Thorpe said only, 'Graham?' but the name held a note of—what? Menace, perhaps, because his brother half turned away, flushing as he muttered, 'As you say, a boy–girl affair doesn't mean much. Still,' with an awkward defiance which wrung Morag's heart with compassion, 'I don't suppose one ever forgets one's first love.'

'It's usually replaced by a second, and later love,' said Morag, speaking to him only.

It seemed that he hesitated for a long moment, his head bent forward so that his expression was hidden, then capitulated completely. 'As you say,' he said, turning to his wife and taking her hand, 'it's replaced by a better and more lasting love. Who was your first love, Louise?'

'A barrow-boy,' she said promptly. 'He had the most delicious apples, and greedy little pig that I was, I adored him. I can remember having a screaming tantrum in the street because my nurse wouldn't buy me one. Fortunately for the good of my character she refused to indulge me, but I've never forgotten him.' She squeezed Graham's hand and said lightly, 'Have you told Thorpe about our decision?'

'No.'

'Then,' she said with determination, 'you'd better do so, my dear. It's been a day of decisions for us too, Thorpe, although ours has been almost made for quite a few weeks. It only needed the news that I'm pregnant to decide us once for all.'

If she had waited to drop her bombshell it was certainly worth it, Morag could not help thinking, for Louise had flung her a triumphant glance as she made her announcement, as if daring her to top that!

Amid the congratulations Morag could not help wondering just what that odd exchange which had preceded it had meant. It was almost as if Thorpe had forced Graham to publicly acknowledge the lies he had told. Then Graham had gone further and prompted by her had surrendered the past completely. Was that, perhaps, the reason for Louise's neurosis, the fact that Graham's jealousy of his brother had prevented him from admitting the lies he had told him, so that he was caught in the web of the past, held there securely by his own inadequacies?

This engagement had, as she had surmised, forced him to accept the fact that Thorpe did not believe him, and with that knowledge there had come release of a sort. Perhaps Louise's condition had helped; whatever had happened, his curt announcement of their decision to move to the Waikato property came as no surprise.

So there was champagne with dinner, a superb meal of spring lamb and Soldier's finest vegetables, followed by Hazel's prize concoction, a *vacherin* of meringue and whipped cream and tiny alpine strawberries which melted in the mouth like summer snow.

'Sumptuous!' Sally sighed from her end of the large baronial table. 'Sandy isn't going to know me when he gets back, I'll be so fat!'

'Nonsense. You're still too thin,' Morag told her crisply, warned by the dark circles under her eyes that the evening's tension had perhaps borne more heavily on Sally than on any one else.

Thorpe—of course—noticed too. 'You'd better have cocoa instead of coffee,' he told his sister. 'And go to bed. You look tired.'

'That's what I love about family,' Sally mourned. 'Such delicacy—such tact! Graham, do I look drear and haggish?'

'Yes,' he said, and laughed at the expression on her face. It was the first time since her return that Morag had heard him laugh, and she was astounded at how young and carefree he looked with the tension smoothed from his features.

Thorpe had been right. If she gained nothing else from this masquerade there would at least be the knowledge that her pain would have brought some happiness for Graham and Louise. Surely once they were away from Wharuaroa and leading their own lives they would be free of the chains which had bound them so tightly.

Unfortunately it seemed as though the bonds which had fastened themselves around her heart were going to be everlasting—there for eternity.

The days that followed were bedlam. Once the notice had appeared in the newspapers there were congratulatory cards and gifts, constant telephone calls and invitations which it would have puzzled Morag to cope with. Fortunately Thorpe dealt with all that, proving such a tower of strength that Morag found herself unashamedly leaning on him, just as Sally did. In some ways he seemed to have changed, too, becoming paradoxically more aloof yet far less arrogant than he had been before. It was bad enough, Morag gloomed, to have fallen in love with the dominating, autocratic despot she had known before, now it seemed that he was reinforcing the ties between them by revealing just how kind and considerate he could be.

He made no attempt to presume on his position as her accepted fiancé. Much to Morag's horror she found herself hoping that he would at least show that he felt some desire for her. When her whole body seemed to become alight as soon as he walked into the room it took all her willpower to convince herself that this new friendliness was far more flattering than the easy passion he had displayed before.

The weather continued fine and warm, the days lengthening out into a spring which had all of the farmers cautiously optimistic for the new season's prospects. A small Cessna aircraft became a permanent speck in the sky, using Wharuaroa's airstrip to spread its white ribbon of fertiliser on the surrounding hills.

'One good thing to come out of World War Two,' Thorpe said, and at Morag's demand for information, told her a little of the saga of aerial topdressing, dreamed up by demobbed pilots who bought old warplanes and had them converted, then set out to convince farmers that they needed their services.

'It saved the farmers an immense amount of work and time each year. In fact, few of these hills would be running sheep or cattle today if it weren't for aerial topdressing,' Thorpe told her. 'Do you want to go up to the strip?'

'I'd love to,' Morag replied, thrilled at the thought of being with him. A pleading glance from Richie made her ask impulsively, 'Could the twins come, too?'

'Yes, of course.'

He seemed cool and offhand about the expedition, but relaxed when the boys promised fervently to be extra good, smiling and ruffling their hair in a way which made Morag realise with aching clarity just how good he would be as a father. That blend of discipline and affection would be ideal—but she caught herself up. To think of such things was dangerous, for she could imagine few greater happinesses than to give him a son or daughter. And if once she started to think like that, she realised shrewdly, it wouldn't be long before she forgot her own precepts and offered him herself, and that way lay disaster. She didn't need any experience of love to know that once she had tasted the ecstasies of passion there would be no other man for her this side of death.

Perhaps she was fooling herself by hoping that if she didn't give in to this love which had sprung unwanted within her it might die a natural death once their paths had separated. But it was the only hope she possessed for anything like happiness in the future.

However, as she settled the twins into the Landrover she didn't care about any forlorn and despairing future. The smile she gave him was one of sheer delight, a delight compounded of the splendid spring day all blue and gold and green, the excitement of the two little boys and above all the pleasure of being with Thorpe. When it was all over, the sapphire back in his safe and she once more in the South Island, she would discover that it was all worth it, she thought. Love, even unrequited love, enriches the lover; she would not allow such a precious emotion to be the cause of any blight on her life. It would be an insult to the way she felt about Thorpe.

'You seem uncommonly pleased with yourself,' he commented, setting the vehicle in motion.

'It's a beautiful day,' she explained, 'and Richie and Jason have promised to be extra well behaved. How could I feel depressed?'

Waiting until the twins' protestations of extreme goodness were over, he said, 'Now if you'd said that part of your pleasure was because you're with me, I'd have taken you out to dinner tonight.'

'Oh!' She pretended to consider, her head on one side. 'What do you think, boys? Shall I tell Uncle Thorpe that I'm happy because he's with us?'

'Yes,' Richie nodded, his bony little face, so like his uncle's, absorbed in the novelty of this method of transport.

Jason was more forthcoming. 'I'm glad you're with us,' he informed his uncle. 'You drive better'n Uncle Graham.'

'No help there,' Morag mourned, meeting a laughing sideways glance from Thorpe. 'So it looks as if I'll have to admit it. I'm very glad you're here.'

'Good girl. I've already booked us a table at the ¿Cuando? in Kerikeri. You'll like it.'

Morag nodded. If Thorpe said she would like it then like it she would. Even if it meant swallowing the fact that he had calmly booked the table without even consulting her, and then made her admit her pleasure in his company.

'No snappish remarks?' he murmured, changing gear as they came to a low rise. 'No crisp comments about my dictatorial methods?'

'Not a one.' She laughed, trying to hide the nervousness which always assailed her when he seemed to read her mind.

'Don't grow too docile. I like you best, I think, with that glint of defiance in your eyes, a diamond within a sapphire.'

'That's only because you like a good fight,' she said flippantly, shaken by the blatant caress in his voice as he spoke.

He grinned, and lifted his shoulders. 'Let's say I prefer to match myself against a worthy adversary,' he returned with smooth conviction. 'Right, hang on, boys, here comes the hairy part!'

Which was a slight exaggeration, for the road, though narrow, was well made and gravelled, and Thorpe was an excellent driver. Nevertheless Morag couldn't help being grateful that he was driving as several of the drops were steep and high enough to make the boys exclaim delightedly.

When at last they reached the airstrip a wide ribbon of vivid green grass running up and over the crest of a hill, the plane was just coming in to land. White and blue, cheerfully unconcerned at the job it had to do, it looked far too small to be carrying the big loads of fertiliser. Not even for Thorpe did it stop. The pilot gave them a V for victory sign, then taxied across to the huge truck which carried the fertiliser from the underground hopper.

They sat in the Landrover, watching as the grey-white dust was pumped into the plane. Then with a sudden deepening in the note of the motors, it was off. Only a few seconds later it lifted from the ground and swooped away, threading its way between the hills with deceptive ease.

Morag, who knew of the casualty rate for topdressing pilots, released a tiny hiss of breath, saying quietly, 'He makes it look so easy.'

'To him it is easy. Well, twins, coming to meet the truck driver?'

Their assent was given in no subdued manner, so Thorpe lifted them down, then, with a gleam in his eyes which she could not meet, lifted Morag too, his fingers tight about her waist as he dropped a careless kiss on the top of her head.

The ready blood mounted to her cheeks, but by the time she had straightened up from pretending to adjust the buckle on her shoe she was once more in control of herself.

Bing Taylor was about as typical a New Zealander as you could find, being tall and lean, with skin burned brown by the sun and the strong jaw which seemed to run in All Blacks and farmers. It was a distinct shock, therefore, when he spoke and revealed himself an Englishman. Morag hoped that her surprise went unnoticed by him; one swift look at Thorpe revealed that he knew exactly how she was reacting and was enjoying it.

As he rolled a cigarette Bing congratulated them both on their engagement, exchanged greetings with the boys, and made a couple of observations about the weather. He and Thorpe spoke briefly about the progress of the topdressing, and then he suggested a trip inside the truck for the boys back to the hopper.

'I should go with them,' said Morag, but she was overborne in the briskest fashion.

'No need, they'll not get into mischief, and we shan't be away for long. Come on, kids!'

The truck roared away, and it was very quiet up there on the grassy hillside, the only sound skylarks singing their ecstasy in the warm blue of the sky. A light breeze touched Morag's arms, bare for the first time that year, and she shivered, more in nervousness than cold.

'Have you got a cardigan?' Thorpe asked.

'No. At least yes, but it's in the Rover and I'm not cold really.'

Stilted words, spoken stiffly, but she could do no better.

'You aren't scared of me,' he said impatiently. 'So give up on the trembling.'

'I am *not* trembling!'

'Ah, that's better.' He laughed softly into her indignant expression and turned her around to face the east, holding her in front of him so that he sheltered her from the breeze. 'There you are,' he said softly, pride vibrating through his tones, 'that's Wharuaroa. What did Wordsworth say? "Earth has not anything to show more fair".'

'Only he spoke about London,' Morag found it difficult to steady her voice.

'Yes. And this is a far cry from any city. Do you like the North, now that you've come back to it and exorcised your ghosts?'

She looked back and up into his face, startled at this incredible perspicacity. 'How did you know I had ghosts to exorcise?'

The muscles of his chest and shoulders moved against her back as he shrugged, 'God knows. A lucky guess, I suppose. You haven't answered my question.'

'It is beautiful. Quite different from my majestic South Island, but it has an appeal entirely of its own. I think I could be brought up here blindfolded and I'd know where I was just from the sounds and the scents, and the soft warmth of the air—Thorpe, it's incredibly clear. Surely I remember a haze?'

'The summer haze.' He bent and kissed her, taking his time about it so that she was breathless when he at last lifted his head, and a pulse beat hastily in the white skin of her throat. 'You're too lovely by far,' he said, an odd thickness softening his voice. 'Small and eminently desirable; capable and shrewish and loving.'

She blinked, still bemused by the touch of his lips on hers and her wanton response to him. 'Shrewish!' she exclaimed, but half-heartedly.

'Yes, shrewish.' He smiled, turning her within the circle of his arms so that she faced him. His glance was piercing, a predatory assessment of the curves and contours of her face, and yet, though she felt the first stirrings of desire which only needed fanning to become a fierce, destroying flame, she also felt that strange security which only he held for her.

'Very shrewish,' he mocked, and kissed her again,

only this time there was little regard for her size or her feelings. His mouth was cruel as it forced her lips to part beneath his and when she would have pushed him away his hands tightened, holding her firmly against him so that every nerve fibre in her body tingled at the hard warmth of his body.

When his mouth lifted she whispered against it, 'Aren't you afraid the truckdriver will see?'

'Bing?' His voice was amused and arrogant at the same time. 'So what? He knows we're engaged. He'd be more surprised by your coldness than by my ardour.'

But he released her and she was left to wonder, for she did not believe that Thorpe usually conducted his amours in the broad light of day in front of an audience. He was a very private man, so secure in the knowledge of his own worth that he did not need to make any effort to be noticed. Nor to attract attention, she thought, remembering the suffocating desire to respond which had been so hard to control. Much more of his lovemaking and she would be in serious trouble.

So she was very distant all the way back and made no particular effort to dress up for the evening. She wished that she had not been beguiled into accepting his invitation, but her common sense came to her aid, telling her that he had already made the reservations before he even asked her, and when Thorpe decided something, few resisted him.

'And that,' she told her reflection, 'sums the whole thing up in a nutshell.'

Which was exactly why she didn't want to spend an intimate evening with him, in case he decided to make use of his prerogative as her fiancé.

Sally appeared in the doorway, looked, and looked again, puzzlement in her eyes.

'Slap me down if I'm speaking out of turn,' she commented, 'but I have seen you look better. Your hair is too scraped back. Here, let me . . .'

Deftly she released Morag's locks from the confining pins, took up the comb and with her head tilted to one side, proceeded to style it carefully.

'It's so lovely and thick, it's a shame to pin it back,' she muttered.

Morag sighed soundlessly. The whole world was against her, it seemed. Although it was flattering to know that Sally would very much like her for a sister-in-law, it meant that she was too eager to make the best of Morag's charms. Of course she didn't realise that the last thing Morag wanted to do was appeal to Thorpe! Not physically, anyway. At least, she corrected herself, not entirely physically. She wanted him to love her, not just desire her, and unfortunately she knew that there was no hope of that. Things had gone wrong for them right from the start. His attitude of recrimination had made her defensive and prickly, and the attraction between them had been reluctant and without any foundation of liking or respect.

Too late now, she mused wearily. It seemed a pity that the one man she had learned to love had to be the only man who had reason to mistrust her, but much she could do about it!

'There, that looks lovely,' Sally purred with satisfaction. 'Now, just a touch more lipstick and you'll look ready to dance till dawn.'

Obediently Morag applied the lipstick, and was rewarded, if reward was the word, by a flickering gleam of appreciation in Thorpe's green-blue eyes when she walked into the drawing room.

It died as soon as it appeared, and it seemed that he had no intention of acting like a lover, at least for the first part of the evening, for in the car on the way down into Kerikeri he was so easy to talk to that she found herself telling him about some of her previous positions. He responded with interest, and for perhaps the first time in their stormy relationship they talked without tension and stress, discussed things like two people who find each other interesting but not antagonistic.

So it was doubly unfortunate that the first people they should have seen once they were inside the ¿Cuando? were Gabrielle and Greg, talking earnestly together in the small cosy bar.

'Why, *Thorpe!*' Gabrielle's expression was illuminated with her delight. 'And Morag too. Come and join us.'

'Don't be insensitive,' Greg scolded her. 'They want to be alone.'

'We'll make an exception for you,' said Thorpe, and Gabrielle's features became radiant again.

Chiding herself for allowing another woman's beauty to rouse her envy, Morag allowed herself to be seated, murmured, 'Sherry,' when Thorpe asked her for her order, and tried to be as natural as she could manage.

At first it was easy enough, because Gabrielle was on her best behaviour. There was none of the overt insolence which had marked her manner before; indeed, she positively radiated good humour, but she could not hide the fact that her attention was almost exclusively bent on Thorpe, as if he filled her horizons to the exclusion of all else.

Wryly Morag admitted that she was human enough to be jealous, even though Thorpe's manner betrayed no trace of anything more than the affection that two friends have for each other. He was very good at suggesting without words that Gabrielle was a charming, beautiful child whom it was a pleasure to be with, but his reserve would have made anyone more sensitive than Gabrielle wary of presuming on their relationship.

At least, that was how it seemed to Morag! Perhaps she was over-sensitive where Thorpe was concerned, or perhaps she was indulging in a little wishful thinking. He had made it quite clear that he felt nothing for Gabrielle; why could she not accept that? Because, Morag admitted gloomily, she was jealous, that was why.

'Gone to sleep?' Greg murmured diffidently.

Starting, Morag shot him a guilty glance. 'Oh dear, I'm sorry. I was thinking.'

'Don't do it,' he said solemnly. 'It never does you any good, I've found. Whenever I've sat down and thought things out logically the result was a disaster. If I follow my impulses I win. Don't think, Morag. Do what your heart tells you.'

He was a dear, and if she had had any sense she would have taken what he offered one night in the clear, crisp air of the Mackenzie high country. But she had refused him bringing her heart back here to have it trampled on by Thorpe.

'I have,' she returned lightly, veiling the clear blue of her eyes with her lashes, for he was too astute.

'Ah yes,' he murmured, one swift glance encompassing the glitter of the sapphire on her finger. 'And yet I'd have thought that happiness would irradiate your features.'

Morag could only be thankful when Gabrielle broke in with a petulant demand to know what they were talking about.

'Reminiscing, my dear girl,' Greg told her, adding with a sly touch of malice, 'I know you didn't really mind,' making it clear that he considered Gabrielle to have been lacking in courtesy.

Gabrielle understood, her vivid beauty dimmed for a moment by anger. After an awkward pause she muttered, 'Of course I don't mind.' Then with a visible effort she turned to Morag, saying as pleasantly as she could manage, 'Thorpe has just told me that Graham and Louise are going to take over the farm in the Waikato.'

There seemed no answer to this, but it was clearly meant as a peace-offering, so Morag responded in kind, aware of Thorpe's indolent glance on her. He was, she thought incredulously, *amused*! How in the name of fortune could she love a man who was so removed from ordinary humankind that he could find a situation like this entertaining! Only someone with no sympathy for human weaknesses and follies could see Gabrielle·trying for dignity and not think more of her for her efforts.

Casting a sparkling glance of dislike at him, Morag set herself out to ease the tension. Oddly enough it seemed that the other girl was willing to follow her lead; Greg's backing was automatic. And Thorpe, although that sardonic amusement was never absent from his eyes, was his usual bland self, so that within a few minutes there was laughter, not all of it forced, from the table and the conversation flowed much more smoothly.

Then Greg drained his glass and said, 'Well, **Gaby** sweet, time we discussed our dinner.'

'Don't *call* me that!' she said automatically, rising with him with obedient swiftness, though her glance lingered on Thorpe a little longer than necessary.

When they were gone Morag lapsed into silence, still angry with him for showing his amusement so clearly.

Others had come into the bar, mostly locals at this time of the year before the tourist rush of summer had set in. Quite a few said 'Good evening' as they passed, or nodded; their womenfolk stole covert looks of interest, about equally divided between Thorpe and his fiancée, Morag was amused to see.

She looked moodily into the amber depths of her glass, then lifted her lashes to peep at him. The warm subdued lighting of the cosy little room could not soften the angular regularity of his features or hide his quite astounding good looks, and the even more astounding fact that his character made those good looks insignificant. The clear sun of spring had deepened his ever-present tan, but touched the copper of his hair with highlights of warm gold, and beneath his dark brows his eyes were the colour of a summer sea. He sat looking down into his drink, and the foreshortening of this view of him emphasised the arrogant line of nose and cheekbones and the strength of the jawline. Morag found that her breath was stifled in her throat as a wave of desire so intense that it rendered her completely at the mercy of her eyes swamped her with its pitiless rush.

He looked up, must have seen something of what she was experiencing, because he smiled, mocking and a little cruel. 'Hardly the time—or the place,' he said, and watched with the eyes of an expert the crimson that flamed suddenly in her cheeks.

'Come on,' he ordered, almost bored, when it became obvious that she was not going to answer.

The waiter materialised, showed them to their table, then left them alone in the intimate dining room, furnished like the rest of the building in Spanish style, with the red-shaded lamps casting a welcome glow over the room.

Looking around, Morag thought that it was a pleasant change from some of the extremely starched restaurants she had been to on other occasions, liked, too, the fact that one helped oneself to whatever one fancied from a vast selection. It was a pity she wasn't hungry, but the food looked so appetising that she found it easy to fill her plate.

Greg and Gabrielle were tucked away in a corner; they waved when Morag and Thorpe returned, but Greg immediately said something to his companion, something outrageous, for she pouted and flashed an answer back at him, and Morag knew then that unless the girl was an excellent actress she was not in love with Thorpe. If Thorpe came into a room where she was sitting, Morag knew, that she could no more switch her attention to another man than fly over the moon. Even when she was talking to someone else she was acutely aware of him; it was as though her skin could see him, she thought fancifully, while he went through the ritual of wine-tasting.

'You seem somewhat subdued now that Greg Layton isn't close enough to be impressed,' he said curtly after the wine-waiter had left them and there had been silence for a few seconds.

Morag felt the skin on the back of her neck prickle with antagonism. 'Don't be silly,' she retorted stiffly. 'I was *not* trying to impress him.'

'It looked remarkably like it.'

She looked up, met the steady coldness of his glance and thought wearily, '*Now* what?'

Aloud she snapped, 'You could hardly have been less helpful!'

'Oh, I could see no reason for interrupting such a talented performance,' he said, and laughed softly at the outrage in her expression. 'You know, you react so perfectly to my teasing I do it just for pleasure! Calm down, I know perfectly well why you became so protective of our *enfant terrible*. You felt sorry for her. Give her credit for discerning your motive. It brought home to her as nothing else could how her behaviour must appear to others. You know, I think this engagement is working out quite well.'

'For you, perhaps,' Morag said pointedly, angry with him for teasing her and with herself for rising to it.

His eyes taunted her with her gracelessness. 'Of course,' he agreed smoothly. 'But your welfare wasn't considered, was it?'

'No.'

He laughed softly, lifted his glass and said with cool insolence, 'Here's to our engagement, then. May it be as profitable for you as it's been for me.'

Morag watched him as he drank, then said crisply, ironically, 'I'm sure it will, you know. It's a pity they changed the law or I could sue you for breach of promise after you decide to call it off.'

'I'd marry you sooner than that,' he said, his expression hardening into a ruthless cruelty that frightened her even though she knew she was safe from it. 'And believe me, if I did you would wish you'd travelled to the end of the earth rather than try to shackle me.'

Fighting off the chill that his words aroused, Morag retorted, 'Well, you needn't worry. As far as I'm concerned you can remain free as an eagle for the rest of your life. It's no concern of mine.'

'No?' he drawled, the hard light fading from his glance.

'No,' she reiterated firmly.

'Then stop being provocative and eat your dinner.'

Which was unfair, but as she attacked some swordfish with a shocking disregard for what she was eating, she decided that it was no use trying to score off Thorpe. He was more than capable of using unfair methods to silence her.

And then he said, quite calmly, 'As a matter of fact, I was going to suggest that there's really no reason why we should break the engagement.'

Morag's fork clattered against the side of the plate as she set it down. 'I *beg* your pardon?' she whispered, shock dilating her eyes.

In the dim light there was a glint of pure devilry in his regard. 'You heard,' he said.

'Why?' she asked, forcing strength into her voice. She was not going to faint, even if he had just opened the doors of paradise to her.

'Because I need a wife,' he answered casually, 'and I'd look a long way before I found anyone as suitable as you.'

'Well, *thank* you!' she retorted sarcastically, wondering how anyone could be so besotted with a man that a proposal so insultingly casual should still manage to invoke a treacherous leap of delight inside her.

He smiled. 'Do you want me to say that I find you desirable? I should have thought I'd made that quite obvious. And I know you're attracted to me. I'm not such a fool as to suggest a marriage of convenience.'

'I wonder that you're such a fool as to suggest any sort of marriage,' she said shakily, angered by his arrogant assumption that she could be swayed by his cold logic. She could not resist adding, 'And it's news to me that I'm in any sort of way suitable for you.'

'At the risk of further offending you, I'll enumerate the ways, if you like.' Taking her silence for assent, he continued mockingly, 'You get on well with Hazel, you're efficient and capable, you perform well in public and you're intelligent. I don't think I'd care to be married to an idiot, however ornamental. You dress well, and when you forget those prickles you can be charming.'

By now Morag had regained some poise, although her heart felt as though it had been wrenched from her body and offered as a sacrifice to some ancient blood-thirsty deity. Couldn't those perspicacious eyes see what he was doing to her?

Aloud she said consideringly, 'I wonder what they'd think if I threw my dinner at you?'

'I shouldn't,' he said, a thread of steel in his voice which warned her that his patience was at an end. 'I don't want an answer immediately. We have plenty of time, but I'd like to make sure your vanity doesn't persuade you to refuse.'

'My *vanity*?' She stared, completely bewildered by this fresh attack on her composure.

'Your vanity.' Reaching across the table, he took her hand, holding it firmly between his in a grip which must look from a distance as if he were indulging in dalliance with her. Only Morag could feel the hardness of his fingers around hers.

'You'd like to bring me to my knees,' he said pleasantly. 'Coax me into falling in love with you. If I'd gilded my proposal with protestations of everlasting adoration you'd have had your ego flattered, and you'd have agreed or taken the utmost pleasure in refusing me. Well, I don't work that way. If you agree to marry me it will be because you want me and because you're too sensible to refuse. I can give you much—and I don't mean material things,' as she made a quick gesture of repudiation. 'I know you're not mercenary. My way of life obviously suits you and in spite of your earlier re-jection of the place, I know you love Wharuaroa, both the homestead and the district. The North suits you, and you belong here.'

She drew a deep breath, almost persuaded by the caressing note in his voice that she could be happy as his wife, even though passion was the main tie that would bind them. Then something in the smile he gave her, some hint of his incredible self-assurance, brought clear cold sanity back to her, and she knew that instead of opening the gates of paradise to her he had offered her a glimpse of hell.

CHAPTER NINE

FOR the rest of her life Morag could never remember what she had eaten during that incredible meal. Greg and Gabrielle came over to say goodbye and she could not recall either of them looking at her strangely—so she must have behaved quite normally.

But she felt distinctly odd, a feeling which was not helped by the glint of appreciation in Thorpe's regard when he finally tucked her into the car after coffee and liqueurs. Perhaps, she thought, she was slightly drunk, and the cold night air was not helping matters. She had certainly had more wine than normal, in part because it helped to ease the aching wound deep inside her. But it had been drunk with a meal, which should have nullified its effect. Certainly she didn't feel tired; indeed her head, though light, was peculiarly clear.

Nevertheless she didn't protest when he drew the car in to the side of the road at the top of the hill and turned it so that it faced back towards the Bay of Islands.

When he cut the engine she said only, 'What are we doing here?'

'Watch,' he murmured.

As her eyes grew accustomed to the darkness she saw the tiny sprinkles of light which were each a window in some farmhouse, and then the collections, Kerikeri half-hidden in shelter belts of eucalypts and bamboo, Russell across the narrow bay on its peninsula, a few brave gleams apparently in the middle of the bay which would be caretakers on the islands. And coming up the harbour, its lights glittering as bravely as a gigantic Christmas tree, was the first liner of the season on its way to the tiny port of Opua at the head of the Bay.

A gentle sigh escaped through Morag's lips. 'Did you know it would be there?' she asked softly.

'It was due tonight.'

That was all, but Morag realised with some astonishment that this man she loved had the sensitivity to know that she would find this sight beautiful and touching in its beauty.

When the lovely thing was lost behind a headland he started the car again without comment, and they drove the rest of the way home without talking. Against her will Morag found herself remembering her old life in Wharuaroa—or perhaps not so much her life as that lived by others such as Lauren. There had been days spent on the sea—skin-diving or water-skiing, followed by a barbecue on a convenient beach and singing around a bonfire, the long summer evenings when it was hot until eight, tramping across the coastal hills or canoeing down the small rivers, sailing—the list was endless, and the long easy days seemed to follow each other like pearls on a string.

This could be hers if she accepted Thorpe's proposal, ease and luxury as well as work, nights of passion and days of contentment. Except that she knew with stark clarity that she could never be content, let alone happy, married to a man whom she loved with all of her heart when he felt nothing more for her than desire and a measure of respect. And she still didn't know whether he really believed her when she protested her innocence against Graham's lies.

'You're very quiet,' he said, when at last they were

inside the homestead. 'Don't tell me that I've at last succeeded in silencing you!'

She met the mockery of his glance with a kind of desperation. 'I've been thinking. Thorpe, I can't——'

'Don't answer me now,' he interrupted, his expression aloof and withdrawn, made hard by its inflexibility.

'It's no use. I can't possibly——'

'*Will* you shut up!' As if angered by her attempts to speak he caught her by the shoulders, staring down into her face, his glance granite-hard. After a moment his scrutiny softened, became lit by the desire she had become so afraid of, and he smiled.

'Don't look so frightened,' he mocked, bending his head to claim her lips as if he had every right to them.

It was a kiss beyond anything she had ever experienced, a sensuous affirmation of masculine power, and something in Morag cast off all the shackles of thought and pride and responded with an ardour which should have shocked her.

But she revelled in the knowledge of her power over him, holding his head with her hands, refusing to allow him to pull away when he lifted his head, though the blaze in his eyes as they rested on her bruised mouth filled her with an exultant terror.

'Morag ...' he muttered, and touched her mouth with his finger, tracing the outline with a gentleness which surprised and thrilled her, then he laughed, and threaded a line of kisses along her jawline, finishing with the closure of his teeth on her earlobe. Like an instrument for his playing she trembled, her body tuned to every change in his, her hands caressing the strength of his shoulders. She did not resist when he slipped the shoulders of her dress down, did not protest when his hand touched her breasts. A wave of desire so intense that she felt helpless beneath its on-slaught swept her from her old life, propelling her into a new realm where only her senses mattered, where the important things were Thorpe's hands and mouth, the masculine need she sensed in him and her own yearning to become his in every possible way, to give him what he so ardently desired, the relief of her body.

Dimly, as his mouth followed the path his hands had made, she knew that she should stop him before it was too late, but his hair was silk between her fingers and she was aflame with a need so urgent it swept away all her principles.

'Thorpe,' she whispered helplessly as he lifted her into his arms, offering her mouth as a willing sacrifice to his passion.

With her signal of surrender the urgency of his desire seemed to recede, become more self-indulgent, almost as if with the need to force a response from her gone he was prepared to woo her into his arms and into his bed. For there could be no doubt that that was where this was leading, and she welcomed the thought with all her heart. Marriage was impossible, but at least she would have the memory of how it felt to lie in his arms, to find an exultation of body and heart which she might never have repeated.

And then, like a douche of freezing water, came the realisation that for him this would be just another incident in a number of such. His very expertise in making love was a clear warning that there had been others in his life who had felt the same abandonment of thought and sense to his mastery of the arts of passion.

'No!' she muttered, as if the word was dragged from her, pulling away so swiftly that she was halfway across the room before she realised that she had moved.

He looked at her, his eyes dark with desire, that

sensuous mouth twisted in an expression of contemptuous appraisal.

'What the *hell* is the matter with you now?' he asked,
the slight slurring of his words revealing just how
powerfully she had affected him.

Morag pulled up the shoulders of her dress, refusing
to turn her back. 'I'm sorry,' she said, shame flooding
her cheeks with colour. 'But I can't.'

'Why?'

Well, she owed him that at least. 'I don't like being
one in a string,' she muttered.

'Bloody hell!' The snarl was reinforced by the glitter
of unnerving rage in his glance as he came towards her,
lean and dangerous as a wild beast balked of its prey.

A pulse beat wildly in Morag's throat, almost preventing her breath. She had the terrifying thought that
she had provoked him too far, that he had so lost control that he would take her by force. Rape was an ugly
word, but she was forced to admit that she would have
brought it on herself by her stupidity. When he reached
her he touched that betraying pulse with a finger
which was cruel in its force. 'You have every reason to
be afraid,' he said softly, half under his breath. 'What
the hell do you want, you cheap little flirt?'

His insult and her own realisation of her foolishness
had the paradoxical effect of stiffening her resolve and
firing her temper. 'I don't want to be used,' she retorted, anger glinting from beneath her lashes.

'You were using me.' The words were flat, as though
he was holding himself on a tight rein, yet they carried
complete conviction.

And Morag hung her head. Unerringly he had
chosen the one remark which she could not defend herself, for if she refuted it she would be admitting that
she loved him.

'Is it love you want?' he demanded harshly, his hands about her throat tilting her chin so that she was forced to look into the implacable anger of his expression. 'Do you want me to tell you that I love you?'

Still she remained mute, her tongue nervously licking her lips.

'Don't *do* that!' he ground out. 'You are the most tantalising, tormenting witch it's ever been my misfortune to want! I can't tell if it's deliberate or if you really are so naïve that you don't know what you're doing.'

'It can't be that, can it?' she asked stiffly. 'Remember me? I'm the scarlet woman who seduced your brother. Only as it happens I'm not all that keen on keeping my favours within the family!'

His fingers tightened mercilessly so that for a moment she thought that he was going to strangle her then and there. But as her head began to whirl he smiled and released her, catching her by the upper arms. 'You've got a vicious tongue,' he said smoothly, apparently once more in control of himself. 'But I detect a certain amount of pique behind your fiery words. Well, do you want me to profess my love with fervour and passion?'

'The seducer's age-old weapon,' she retorted, mustering up all the scorn she could call on. 'You needn't bother, Thorpe, I wouldn't believe you—and I'm not going to allow a situation like this to develop again.'

'You can't stop it,' he said dangerously. 'Because in spite of that lump of ice you call a heart you want me. It's as simple as that. And once you've admitted it to yourself and allowed yourself to defrost you'll be surprised at how simple it is.'

Bitterness roughened her voice. 'I know how simple it is. So—I do want you: I admit it. But I refuse to—

to behave like a trollop just because of that!'

'Oh—Morag!' His smile was twisted, ironic yet oddly gentle. 'You make me so angry that I could beat you, then you disarm me equally easily. I don't believe that you and Graham had any other relationship than the most innocuous.'

Astounded, she looked up, searching his face for the truth.

'Why?' she asked.

'Let's say that I've enough experience to know. Also,' with a sudden glitter of dislike which made her draw her breath in sharply, 'when Graham realised what our engagement meant, that either I didn't believe him or didn't care, he told me the truth.'

'I see.' She should be glad, of course, but all she could think of was that he had not trusted her at all, relying on his own expertise and Graham's admission. Stifling a pang of desolation, she continued, 'Did he tell you why he'd lied both to you and to Louise?'

'Yes.' He released her arms, gesturing towards a seat. 'Sit down. It's all right, you've managed to avert whatever punishment I had in mind for you.' Waiting until she was seated he poured two brandies and gave her one, saying with a return of his old impatience when she shook her head, 'Don't be silly. I don't make women drunk in order to seduce them.'

Warily she sipped the drink, watching as he stood across the room from her, slightly turned away so that all she could see of him was a black profile and the springy strength of his frame.

After a moment he said, 'He lied to me because he thought I was so stuffed with old-fashioned conventions that I'd insist on a marriage. Unfortunately for his scheme,' with a glimmer of a smile, 'he knew remarkably little of me. As far as Louise is concerned—

well, you've seen how the situation is with them. She was astute enough to realise that you had meant something to him; when she taxed him with it he said he wanted to make her jealous.'

'You told me that she was almost pathologically jealous already.'

He nodded, turning to look squarely at her. 'The story of Graham's life, I'm afraid. He just doesn't understand any other person.'

Morag had to ask it. 'Do you think this move will help them?'

'I don't know,' he said heavily. 'At least it won't make things worse. I've done all I can for them. From now on it's up to them. Louise, I think, in spite of her behaviour, is the more stable of the two. If she can straighten up there's hope for them both. But it's up to them now.'

Morag nodded, keenly aware of the unspoken worry that lay behind his words of dismissal. Poor Thorpe, she thought compassionately. So much depended on him, the welfare of Wharuaroa and several other properties and all the people who worked on them, and then the worry of his family as well as all the natural disasters that are the lot of farmers everywhere. His shoulders were broad enough to take them, but she realised for the first time why he had said that he needed a wife. Even if there was no great love between them it would probably be a relief for him to be able to discuss things with an interested, intelligent companion. No one could be as self-sufficient as he appeared. And if that companionship was spiced with passion so much the better, she thought wryly.

Afraid that her sympathy was weakening her resolve to stand firm against his insidious attacks on her defences, she put the barely touched brandy down, saying crisply, 'I suppose all anyone can do is hope they survive. Do you mind if I go to bed now, Thorpe? I'm tired.'

'No doubt,' he mocked, but not with any particular unkindness. Indeed he seemed glad rather than irritated by her retirement, escorting her to her room with a preoccupied air which she found intensely irritating.

So much for logic, she reflected sadly as she creamed the make-up from her face. Instead of being pleased at his aloofness she chose to be angry about it!

The weather had closed in by morning, being cool and wet, the garden a rainswept oasis sheltered from the brisk westerly which tossed the totaras in the paddock and sent the flocks of gulls which had flown inland soaring and wheeling above the paddocks.

Richie woke up fretful and hot; an inspection by a suspicious Morag revealed ominous spots on his trunk and a call went out to Dr Griffiths.

When she arrived it was late in the evening and Jason had joined his brother in the nursery, fractious, flushed and unco-operative.

'Yes, chickenpox!' the elderly doctor said, eyeing Sally sympathetically. 'Not too bad, my dear. They'll be fine in a few days. How are you?'

'Ill at the thought,' Sally groaned. 'But physically fine.'

Smiling, the doctor turned to Morag. 'I'm glad you're here,' she said briskly. 'You'll be able to stop this nitwit from worrying herself sick, and Thorpe will be able to call a halt if you look like running yourself ragged. Ever coped with chickenpox before?'

'You name it, I've coped with it,' Morag told her, liking her immensely. 'I know the drill, I think. Keep them quiet, plenty to drink and stop them scratching.'

'I'll send up some lotion for that.' The doctor turned to Sally, evidently confident of Morag's skill. 'You just do what you're told to do, my dear, and no worrying about your share of the work. Hazel and Miss Nelson will cope without you wearing yourself out.'

If the following nightmarish days had any benefit at all it was that they were too busy to give Morag any time to think! For Sally came out with the ominous-looking spots and was sicker by far than her sons, lying weak and exhausted-looking in her bed for days after they were on their feet. Hazel helped, but the cooking and housekeeping was a full-time job for her, especially concocting delicacies to tempt Sally's appetite, so aid from her was limited.

Thorpe sat with his sister, teased her gently and made her laugh. He was wonderfully patient with her, Morag thought, for a man who was so very impatient.

One day, when the sun had re-emerged after days of sulking behind rainclouds, Morag went for a quick walk in the garden, breathing deeply of the fresh, warm air. The shelter belts protected the garden from damage by wind, but the rain had browned the last few camellias. Sadly, their season was over, but on a huge rose bush which rambled over a rustic pergola there were leaves and two exquisite pink blooms, pointing the way to summer. Soon, she thought, the hibiscus would be out, their petals like silken bells in the garden, and with them would come all the summer flowers, the vivid lilac blue of the jacarandas, the soft candy-floss of the silk tree and the lovely pink and white orchid flowers of the bauhinias. The beds would be gay with sweet william and verbena and daisies with gladioli as accents and the white heads of alyssum among the cottage pinks which were another of Soldier's favourite flowers.

Yes, summer would be lovely in this garden, she mused, coming to a halt by the swimming pool. It couldn't be very old, that pool, but it blended beautifully with its surroundings. The split sandstone flagging gave it a pleasantly formal informality and at one end was a cabana where there were dressing rooms and a big sitting area as well as a barbecue under a pepper tree. When the days lengthened Soldier would shift the chairs and tables out and the lucky people who lived here would be able to stretch out and get an early tan.

But she would not be here. Each day that passed deepened her love for Thorpe, but hardened her resolve not to give in to the treacherous promptings of her heart. Better the quick clean break than the gradual loss of any hope of happiness, withered by the fact that Thorpe could not love her. At least that way her memories would be ones to treasure, not bitter regrets.

When she turned from the glittering expanse to go back into the house it was to almost bump into Louise, standing straight behind her.

'I'm sorry!' Morag gasped, nearly overbalancing in her efforts to avoid the other girl.

'My fault.' The crisp clear tones were devoid of emotion. 'I want to see you. We'll talk here.'

What now? Morag thought, but allowed herself to be piloted to a seat under the golden heart-shaped leaves of the catalpa tree.

Once seated Louise began as though she had planned exactly what to say. 'I think you've had your time here made unnecessarily awkward because of my husband.'

She paused as though waiting for an answer. But Morag did not know how to answer this, so contented herself with a noncommittal noise.

'He's jealous of Thorpe, of course,' Louise resumed after a moment. 'I think that Thorpe was like his father and was made much of because of that, by both his mother and his father. Graham grew up feeling the odd one out. I've seen it happen before.'

For the first time the unnatural calm seemed to tilt a little. In a voice less like a recording, Louise said swiftly, 'I came to apologise. Graham will not; he hates to be found out in his lies, but it doesn't seem fair for us to go without my trying to set the record straight.'

'I see.' Morag blinked, feeling inadequate. 'That's very—very thoughtful of you.'

The beautifully smooth blonde head tilted. Morag felt the gaze from behind the dark glasses fixed on her face.

'It's for the best, I think,' Louise said after a moment. 'It isn't good for Graham to be here, eating his heart out for all he feels he's been deprived of. I think he'll be happier away from here.' She looked around and sighed.

It was the sigh which broke through Morag's reserve. Impulsively she asked, 'Will you be happier?'

Louise looked steadily at her. 'I love my husband,' she answered with a bleak smile. 'Weak as he is, he's mine. He relied on me. I wanted him to be like Thorpe, strong and masterful, always confident, but he can't be. It took you to make me realise that.'

'Me?' Morag's astonishment was patent.

Louise smiled. 'Yes. When we met in England Graham behaved like Thorpe. I thought he was the strong one. Then we came here and Graham shrivelled, and I saw him for what he is. And I hated—oh, not him, but the lie he'd lived for me. I was cruel to him. And I hated Thorpe for being all that Graham is not. And then you came.'

A riro-riro warbled its soft plaintive notes, the shy grey warbler, tiniest bird in the New Zealand bush, bashful harbinger of rain. From a big pink flag lily a bumble bee crawled forth, liberally sprinkled with pollen. It was very quiet.

Louise went on, 'I knew immediately that something had happened between you and Graham. He looked guilty yet exultant, as though he'd found something important. And when I pressed him he told me—what he told me—and I went to Thorpe. But Thorpe wouldn't promise to send you away, and I could guess why.'

'Louise——' Morag suddenly felt that she could not bear any more of these confidences. They were too painful, dragged as they were from the depths of the woman's reticence.

'Please! We're to be sisters-in-law. It's best that we try to come to some sort of understanding. In his own way Thorpe has been kind to me, and I think Graham is fonder of his brother than he dares to admit. I don't want all channels of communication cut.'

'You're a courageous woman,' Morag said with tentative respect.

Louise smiled faintly, but a faint flush on those high, smooth cheekbones showed that the compliment was appreciated. 'I've been behaving like a fool,' she confessed reluctantly. 'Worse than that. In a way I caused Graham's lies. If it hadn't been for the way I was behaving he would not have tried to make me jealous. I was so wrapped up in my own unhappiness and resentment that I wanted you to go so that I could go on blaming Graham for tricking me and making us unhappy.'

'I think you're too harsh on yourself,' Morag protested.

'Oh no. I even spied on you—you and Thorpe. I

felt smirched by my guilt for that.' Louise moved rest-lessly, then swallowed. 'I saw I must go. I wanted to leave Graham, but I couldn't. He needs me, and I love him too much to leave him alone with his demons. So then I realised that we both must go. When you an-nounced your engagement I knew it was the time to make the break. I used you to persuade Graham, saying that I couldn't bear to be here with you. He didn't want to leave Wharuaroa, so he told me the truth, that there'd been nothing between you except an innocent affair. I knew it was the truth. But I pretended to dis-believe him, and he gave in. My methods are not, per-haps, in the best of taste, but at least they were for a good objective.'

'I hope you'll find your happiness,' Morag said gently.

'They say that happiness eludes you if you search for it. So I'll just tell myself that I'm happy and hope that my head convinces my heart. At least things are more settled now. I no longer blame Graham for his weak-nesses; how can I when my own are so glaring? And what he did, he did to win me. And there's the baby.'

She appeared to derive considerable comfort from this thought, rising to her feet with the studied grace which was so essential a part of her. As she did she re-moved her sunglasses and smiled, revealing eyes which were still watchful but free from the turmoil and in-security which had been so noticeable before.

'Thank you for coming to talk to me,' said Morag, suddenly wishing that she could get to know her bet-ter.

'It wouldn't have been fair to go without clearing things up,' said Louise. 'We leave on Thursday, you know.'

'Is there anything we can do?'

'With Sally still so sick? No, thank you, I've got a firm of professional packers to move us and three of the shepherds' wives are going to scrub the house out after we've gone. Thorpe has invited us to dinner the night before, so we'll see you then. Until then—goodbye.'

'Goodbye.'

When she had gone Morag found herself hoping fervently that for Louise and Graham the Waikato would provide the stepping stone to a happiness more real and enduring than any they had known so far, based as it would be on honesty, of a sort, she thought. Perhaps Louise would never be able to be completely honest with Graham; he would be a man who might always need managing. A horrible term, Morag thought, frowning, but Louise was the stronger of the two and the only woman who could give him peace of mind. Yes, for Louise and Graham there was hope.

Thinking deeply, she made her way back to the house, to be met by Hazel. 'They're all still asleep, so why don't you go for a walk? A good brisk one to bring some colour back to your cheeks. Go down by the yards if you want to see some action, they're drafting cattle.'

'Dust and dogs and swearing,' said Morag with a sly smile. 'The last person they'll want is a female to cramp their style.'

'Go on,' Hazel chuckled. 'I know one who'll be pleased to see you anyway. He's been taking your absence hard. Very grumpy lately, our Thorpe.'

Morag was aware that her smile at this sally was a pale imitation of what a smile should be, but she could not summon up the energy to be convincing. If Hazel only knew...!'

Nevertheless she found her footsteps taking her down the hill towards the yards where a mob of huge red stud Herefords were milling around. There was no dust as the sun was not strong enough to dry out the puddles left by the preceding day's rain, but the mud was a fair substitute and there was certainly enough barking from the dogs, bawling from the cattle and yelling from the men to make a picturesque scene.

Thorpe was there, of course, in the thick of things. Morag climbed the high side of an empty pen, wrinkling her nose slightly at the smell as she eased her seat on to the warm, slightly damp wood. From there her view was excellent. None of the men had seen her yet, so preoccupied with their work were they, but she ticked them off. Young Grant Flower, the two brothers, Tim and Tom Hall and nuggety Sam Greenbank, as well as Hazel's Soldier. And Thorpe who dominated the rest by sheer force of personality.

And then, as she began to relax, it happened—quite out of the blue, so swiftly that she did not realise what was happening until it was almost too late.

Thorpe was the only one in the pen; he turned to the side and called out something to Sam in the next pen. Morag could see the gleam of his teeth in the tanned skin of his face as he grinned. From the gate at the other end of the pen a beast erupted, young and fast and vicious, with Thorpe very obviously in his sights.

She screamed, 'Thorpe—*behind you!*' but he seemed to freeze, though he turned to face the animal. Perhaps she screamed again, she could never remember, but one of the men yelled an obscenity, and then when the animal was only a yard away from Thorpe, its head down for the final thrust, he vaulted sideways and was up the wall of the pen before the animal had skidded to a stop.

Morag thought she was going to faint. The trees and

the sky whirled hideously around her head for long
seconds, then steadied down. Pulses hammering, she
climbed very carefully down the rails, slipping into
Thorpe's arms as if she belonged there.

And scanning the concerned eyes that searched her
face, she burst out, 'You *bloody* fool,' she sobbed. 'You
could have been killed! I thought it had you!'

To her horror open tears were running down her
cheeks; of their own volition, her hands were touching
every strong feature as though only by touch could she
reassure herself that he was there.

'Hey!' he said on an expelled breath. 'You should
know that the only way to deal with a charging animal
is to wait until it closes its eyes for the charge and then
move sideways. Morag—listen to me!'

'I thought you c-couldn't move,' she wept, refusing
to be comforted by his cold logic. 'I thought it was going to k-kill you.'

'My poor little love,' he said into her hair as he
pulled her close to him. 'Darling, I'm sorry you were
so frightened, but at least you know now that I can
cope with wild bulls!'

The thread of amusement in his voice, allied to the
casual endearments, fanned the latent flames of her
anger.

'I don't care,' she choked, groping for a handkerchief
to dry her eyes. 'I don't care what you do. I don't care
if you play matador with a thousand bulls——'

'Ah, but you've just proved that you *do* care,' he said,
sounding extremely smug. 'And as it took the bull to
break through those icy defences you erected so carefully around yourself he can look forward to a ripe old
age on Wharuaroa.'

Very carefully she blew her nose and wiped her eyes,
refusing to look up at him as the enormity of what she

had revealed by her injudicious reaction to his danger broke upon her. Held like this in the warm strength of his arms it was hard to think objectively, especially as she could tell by his heightened heartbeat that the adrenalin was still pumping through his veins. Hers too, for that matter, she thought, feeling the thunder of her pulses in her ears.

As if impatient at her delaying tactics he tipped her chin up, gave her a long, considering scrutiny, and then bent his head and kissed her firmly, taking his time about it.

'And that's enough sideshow for the men,' he said against her mouth. 'I'll take you up to the house.'

'No,' she blurted out, adding quickly, 'You've still got work to do, haven't you?'

'They can get on without me for a few minutes,' he said blandly. 'Now that those defences have been breached I'm not going to run the risk of you doing a quick repair job.'

It was only a few hundred yards from the house, but he insisted on taking her up in the Landrover. Probably it was just as well, she conceded, for her legs felt distinctly odd at the knees and she couldn't think objectively; she was still too strung-up by his narrow escape.

Hazel met them, gave one concerned look at Morag's white face and began to offer cups of tea.

'She needs a drink,' said Thorpe, brusquely. 'Make tea by all means, but I'll give her a brandy first.'

He took her into the study, gave her brandy and poured himself a very small one, saying with a return to his autocratic ways, 'Come on, drink up. You've had quite a shock.'

Warily, miserably conscious that now he knew of her love he was in a position of power, she sipped at the liquid, welcoming the comforting glow as it warmed her limbs.

'That's better,' he observed. 'The colour's coming back into your face.' As if he too was unsure of his ground he walked across to the window, stared out into the warmth of the spring day, then turned, a silhouette against the golden light outside.

Very quietly he said, 'Why have you been so careful not to let me see how you feel, Morag?'

When she made no answer his voice hardened. 'You do love me, don't you?'

Nervously she licked her lips, aware that he could see every shade of emotion in her expression, whereas he was a shadow. After a long tense moment she asked defiantly, 'Does it matter?'

'*Matter?* Of course it matters, you stubborn, bad-tempered *idiot*!' Impelled by his anger he came across the room like a tiger, hauled her up from her chair and stared down into her closed face, his fingers hard on her arms.

'It matters,' he said, speaking slowly and clearly as if she were a particularly dense child and he barely able to contain his temper, 'It matters very much because I rather think I've been in love with you since you were seventeen. Why else would I have kept you here against my better judgment, used Louise's neurotic fears to force you into my arms and been so jealous of Greg Whatsisname that I forced you into this engagement? You must have known when I asked you to marry me! Morag, why are you *crying*, for Pete's sake?'

His exasperation was palpable, but Morag, who never wept, for the second time in an hour could not stop herself. 'Why didn't you tell me?' she whispered. 'I've been so unhappy.'

'Why didn't I tell you? Heaven help me! A man needs some encouragement, and all you've done is snap and snarl, making it quite obvious that as far as you were concerned I was a sort of Simon Legree. If it weren't for the fact that you melted into my arms so exquisitely whenever I kissed you I'd have given up hope long ago.'

'Oh—*Thorpe*,' she sighed blissfully, lifting her head from the comforting warmth of his shoulder. 'We've been such idiots! I must have loved you almost from the beginning, because——' But her confession was lost in the demanding pressure of his mouth on hers, which brought on an eruption of feeling, a combination of the after-effects of her terror and the joy of knowing that he loved her, so intense that she could only cling to him in wordless surrender, her whole being caught up in a rapture which made all that had gone before pale into insignificance.

After a timeless time, when all that mattered was the sight and scent and feel of him, he said, his voice roughened by passion, 'If I know Hazel she'll have decided that it's about time you had that tea. Now make yourself respectable, or I'll forget I have a mob of cattle waiting for me and deal with you as I want to.'

'I thought you had,' she said mistily, still bemused.

His eyes darkened and the curve of his mouth deepened into something almost threatening. 'No, my heart, that can wait until our honeymoon. But we'd better get married soon.'

'We can't,' she said. 'There's poor Sally, and she'll want her husband here——'

'Then I won't be responsible for your continued purity,' he said softly, stopping her from buttoning up her blouse by the simple expedient of kissing the hollow between her breasts.

She laughed, and held his head away from her, caressing the lines and planes of his face. 'I don't care,' she returned.

'Don't you? The same way you didn't care about the bull?' he smiled, and pulled her to her feet. 'You're right, of course. We'll wait. I've waited six years for you, a couple of months won't make much difference.'

'Truly?'

'Truly.' He held her close, kissed the top of her head. 'You impressed me right from the start, the one kid in the valley I noticed. And how I noticed you! It irked me, but I didn't think much about it until Graham dropped his bombshell. I suddenly felt smirched, as though something I loved had been desecrated. That's why I was so brutal when I paid you off.'

Morag nodded into his shoulder, the incident surfacing from her memory in its usual clarity. She had hated him, but she had never forgotten him and his power and authority had impressed her in spite of her hatred.

'Then I tried to forget you, but your cheques kept arriving—such little ones, as though they were being saved with difficulty!' His voice was raw, his kiss on her cheek very tender. 'I felt a heel and I told myself that just because you had no morals it didn't necessarily apply to other areas of your life. After a while I found myself making excuses for you—you were so young. And still I didn't realise what you'd done to me.

'When did you?' she asked lovingly.

'When I saw you at the airport. My eyes met yours, and I felt a shock of raw desire. I knew then that I wasn't going to get you out of my system unless I purged myself from wanting you, and there was only one way to do that. And Louise provided me with the perfect opening.'

Morag nodded, somehow not in the least surprised that he had been so direct in his appreciation of the situation. She had always known that he wanted her, she had thought herself safe from him while she was in his home, but apparently she had been wrong, if he meant what she thought he did.

Swiftly she told him some of what had passed between Louise and herself, only revealing what she thought Louise would not object to.

'I hope things work out,' he said after a moment. 'Just now I want everyone to be as happy as I am.'

'Me, too.'

'We've waited long enough,' he said with a return of his old arrogance. 'Your fault, my darling.'

'No, yours! If you hadn't made it so obvious that you despised me I'd probably have given the show away much sooner.'

'It was my only defence. I knew—oh, the night that Louise came back and found you in my arms—that it was more than a physical need I felt for you, but you so clearly resented what you considered to be your weakness towards me that I had to keep stressing the ties. Then Greg turned up and I could have killed you, you were so obviously relaxed and friendly with him, so I walked the floor and concocted the engagement scheme, manufacturing as many reasons as I could to convince you it was a good thing. I had every intention of marrying you by then.'

'So you were as nasty to me as you possibly could be!'

He grinned, apparently not in the least ashamed of his behaviour. 'What else could I do? The only way I could get to you was by angering you or making love, and quite frankly I didn't know I could stop if once I started loving you! Oh, my love,' his voice roughened into a longing so intense that she shook with the desire to assuage it, 'you've led me such a dance, but it was all worth it, just for this moment. I do love you so much!'

They were married on the first day of summer in the little church at Kerikeri.

The citrus orchards were in full flower and the perfume of orange blossom permeated the air, exotic yet familiar. Morag carried white carnations, tiny white gladioli and orange blossom, and wore the traditional white gown, but when she walked up the aisle to where Thorpe stood waiting for her it was not her gown which drew people's eyes but the radiance of her expression, and those who saw Thorpe when he turned to greet her felt the age-old ache of longing that such happiness might be theirs eternally.

And afterwards, when the twins had dutifully given the bride a horseshoe and what Thorpe called the 'whole paraphernalia of the reception' was over they left Wharuaroa and slipped down towards the coast, embarking at Paihia for one of the little islands in the beautiful Bay. It belonged to a friend of Thorpe's, a friend who was delighted to lend it to them for their honeymoon.

'Which one is it?' Morag asked, still not entirely at ease with her new husband.

'Not very far now.' He made no effort to touch her in front of the tall, thin, elderly man who had come to get them and who was the caretaker. 'There, you can see it coming into sight now.'

They had a guest cottage in the grounds of the big house, and that night, when the summer stars were blazing in a sky of blue-black velvet, Morag learned of the ecstasy which comes when passion is transformed into something beyond desire, a unity of heart, mind and body which at the same time sated and yet promised more.

Then she knew that the lonely days were past. When she told Thorpe of this, her voice hesitant in the dim light of the starlit room, he tightened his arms around her slim body and said, the words almost a vow, 'Believe me, sweet, they're gone for ever. Whatever happens, we're together.'

And even as his mouth sought hers and she gave herself up to their need for each other she thought that she could ask nothing more of life than their love, so hardly won, so reluctantly given and so doubly precious.

ANNOUNCING

Masquerade

SEPTEMBER TITLES

THE EMPEROR'S JEWEL
by Lisa Montague

How could Sophie — Napoleon Bonaparte's beloved
ward, the Emperor's Jewel — fall in love with
Edmund Apsley, an English spy? It was unthinkable,
but it was true.

BLACK FOX
by Kate Buchan

A king's word can create an alliance — but not love,
and Isabel Douglass is determined to escape an
arranged marriage with the fierce, proud Master of
Glencarnie who regards her with open contempt as a
mere political pawn. Yet a Fate stronger than either
seems to draw them inexorably together . . . .

NOVELS OF ROMANCE INTRIGUE AND EXCITEMENT

Forthcoming Classic Romances

A GIRL ALONE
by Lilian Peake

Sparks had flown between Lorraine Ferrers and Alan Darby from the moment they met — and it was all Lorraine's fault, for not trying to conceal her prejudice against him. Then, unwillingly, she found herself falling in love with him — but hadn't she left it a little late?

JAKE HOWARD'S WIFE
by Anne Mather

Jake Howard was immensely attractive, immensely rich, immensely successful. His wife Helen was beautiful, intelligent, well bred. A perfect couple, in fact, and a perfect marriage, everyone said. But everyone was wrong . . .

A QUESTION OF MARRIAGE
by Rachel Lindsay

Beth was brokenhearted when Danny Harding let her down, and vowed that it would be a long time before she fell in love again. But fall in love again she did — with Danny's cousin Dean, a very different type of man indeed, and one who really loved her. Or did he? Surely fate wouldn't be so cruel as to strike Beth again in the same way?

WHISPERING PALMS
by Rosalind Brett

The discovery of mineral deposits on her African farm came just at the right time for Lesley, but besides prosperity, it brought a scheming sister determined to get most of the spoils herself and to marry the most eligible bachelor in Central Africa.

Mills & Boon Classic Romances

— all that's best in Romantic Reading

Available October 1979

☐ GT51
COME BLOSSOM-TIME, MY LOVE
Essie Summers

☐ GT52
WHISPER OF DOUBT
Andrea Blake

☐ GT53
THE CRUISE TO CURACAO
Belinda Dell

☐ GT54
THE SOPHISTICATED URCHIN
Rosalie Henaghan

☐ GT55
LUCY LAMB
Sara Seale

☐ GT56
THE MASTER OF TAWHAI
Essie Summers

☐ GT57
ERRANT BRIDE
Elizabeth Ashton

☐ GT58
THE DOCTOR'S DAUGHTERS
Anne Weale

☐ GT59
ENCHANTED AUTUMN
Mary Whistler

☐ GT60
THE EMERALD CUCKOO
Gwen Westwood